FANTASTICA
The World of Elements

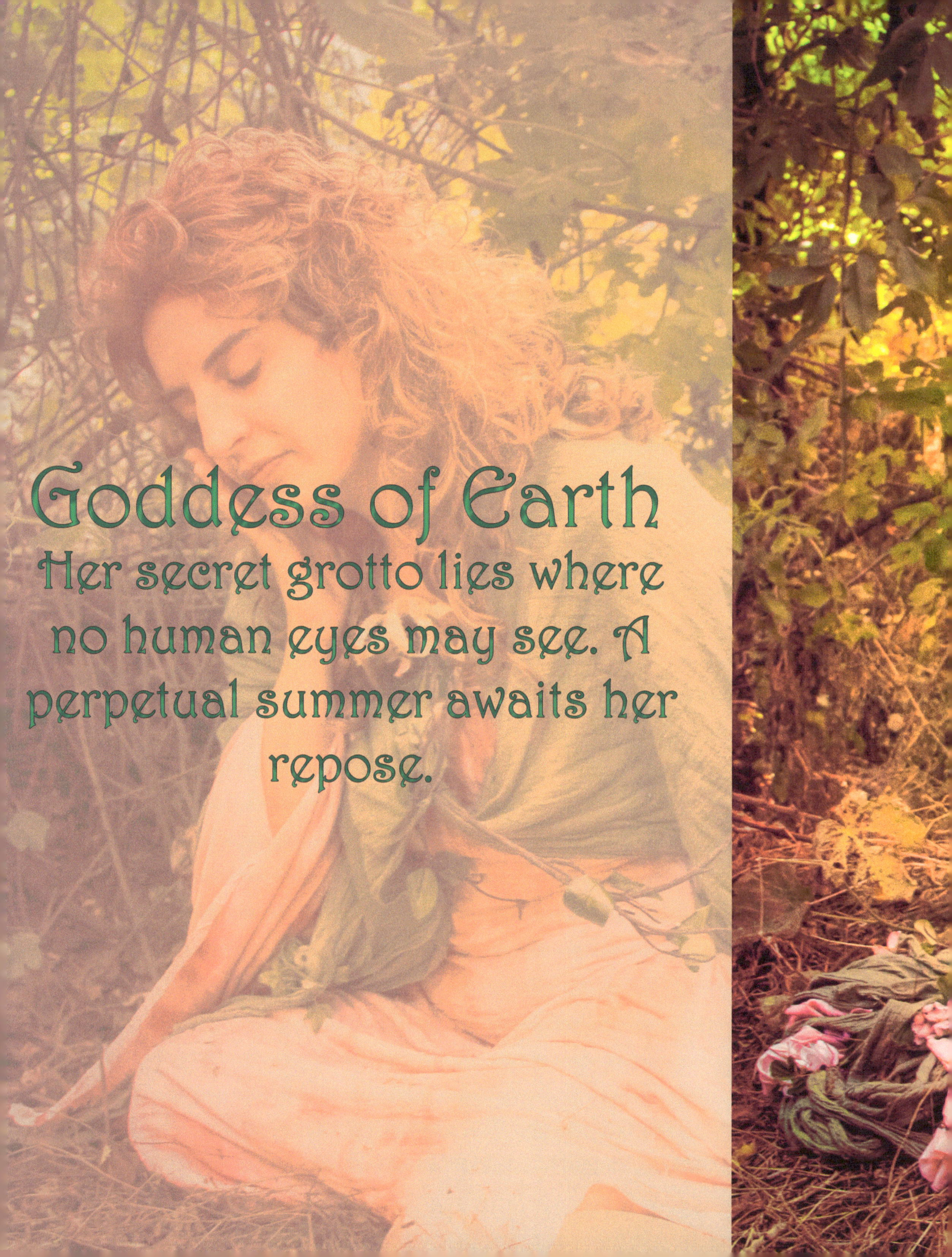

Goddess of Earth
Her secret grotto lies where no human eyes may see. A perpetual summer awaits her repose.

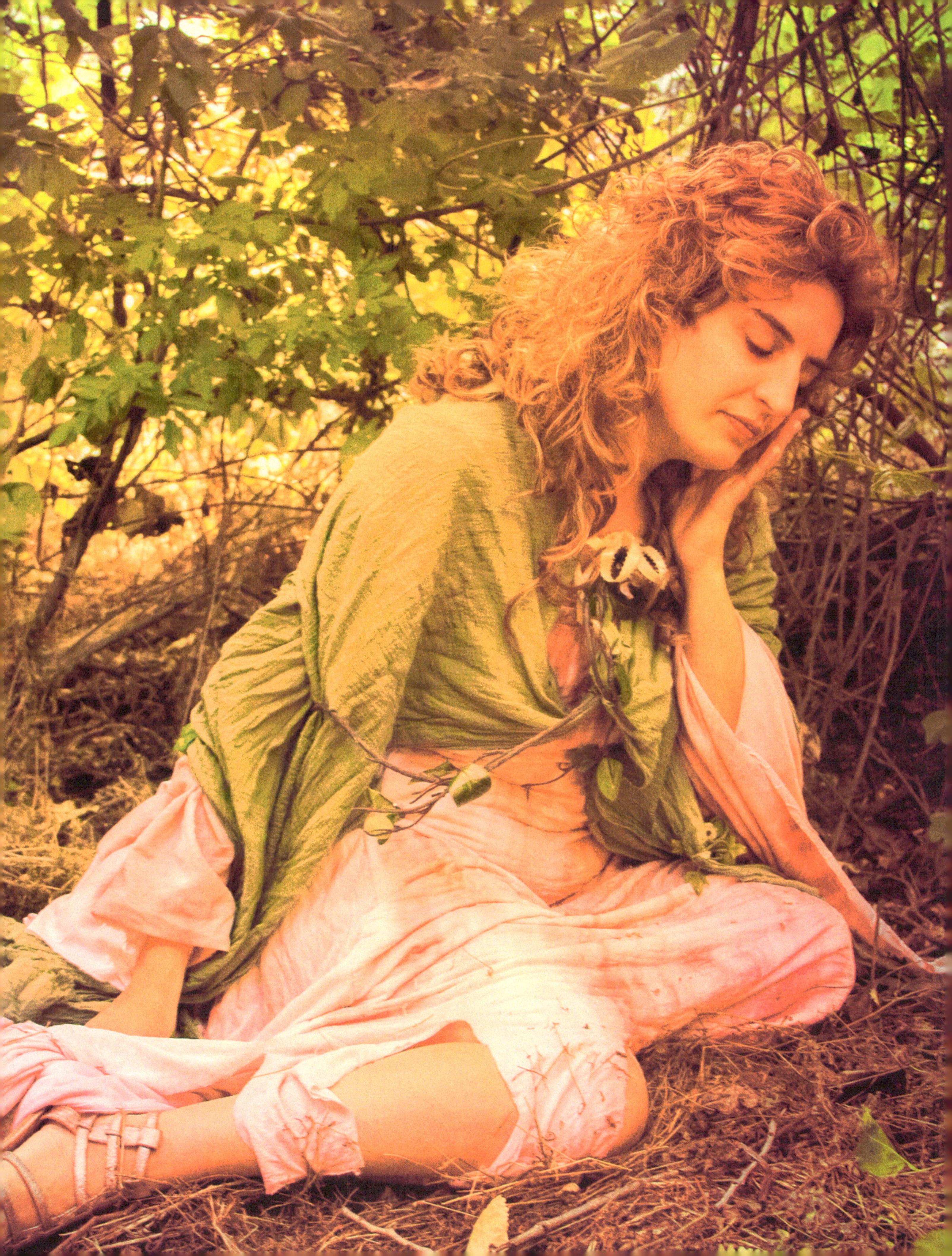

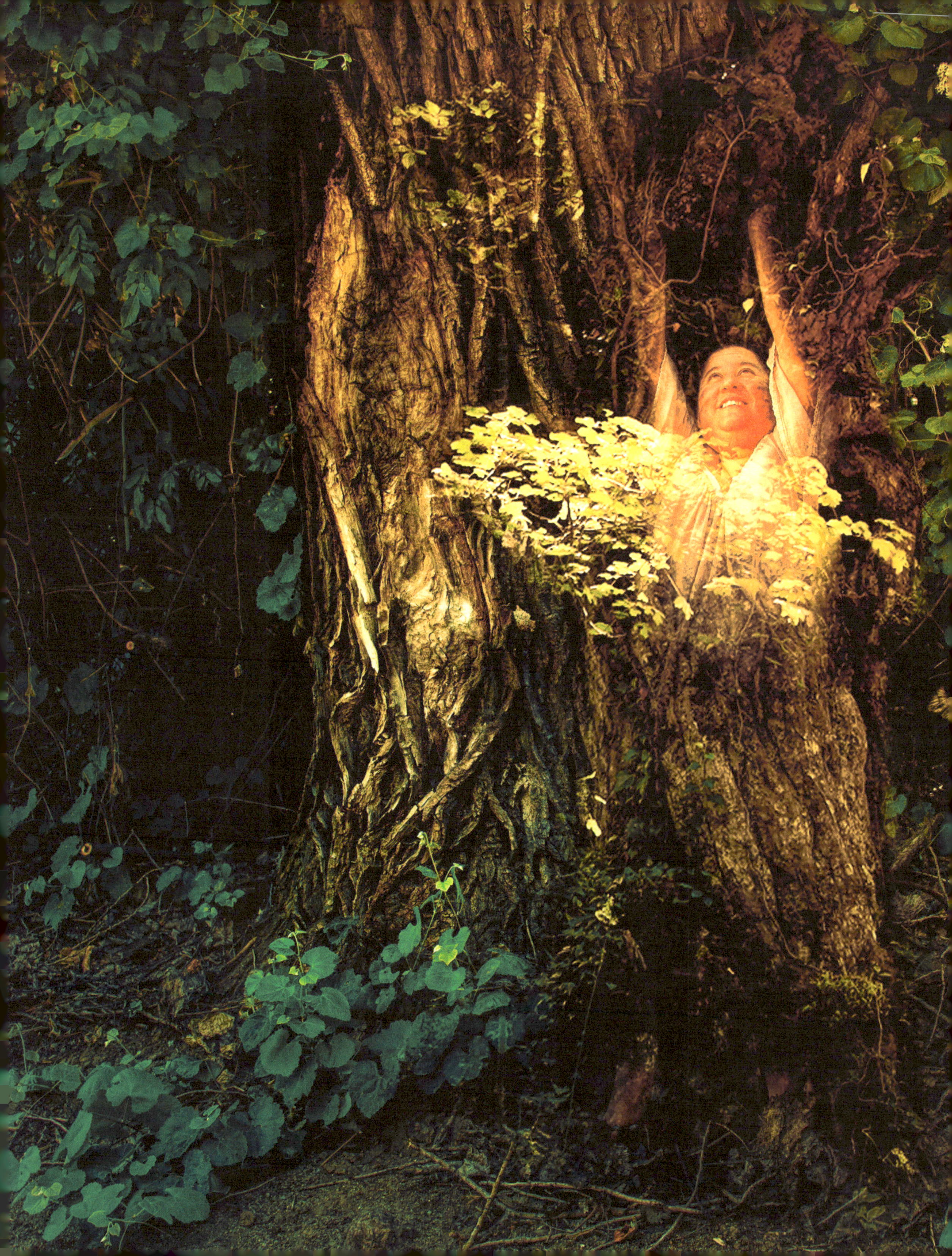

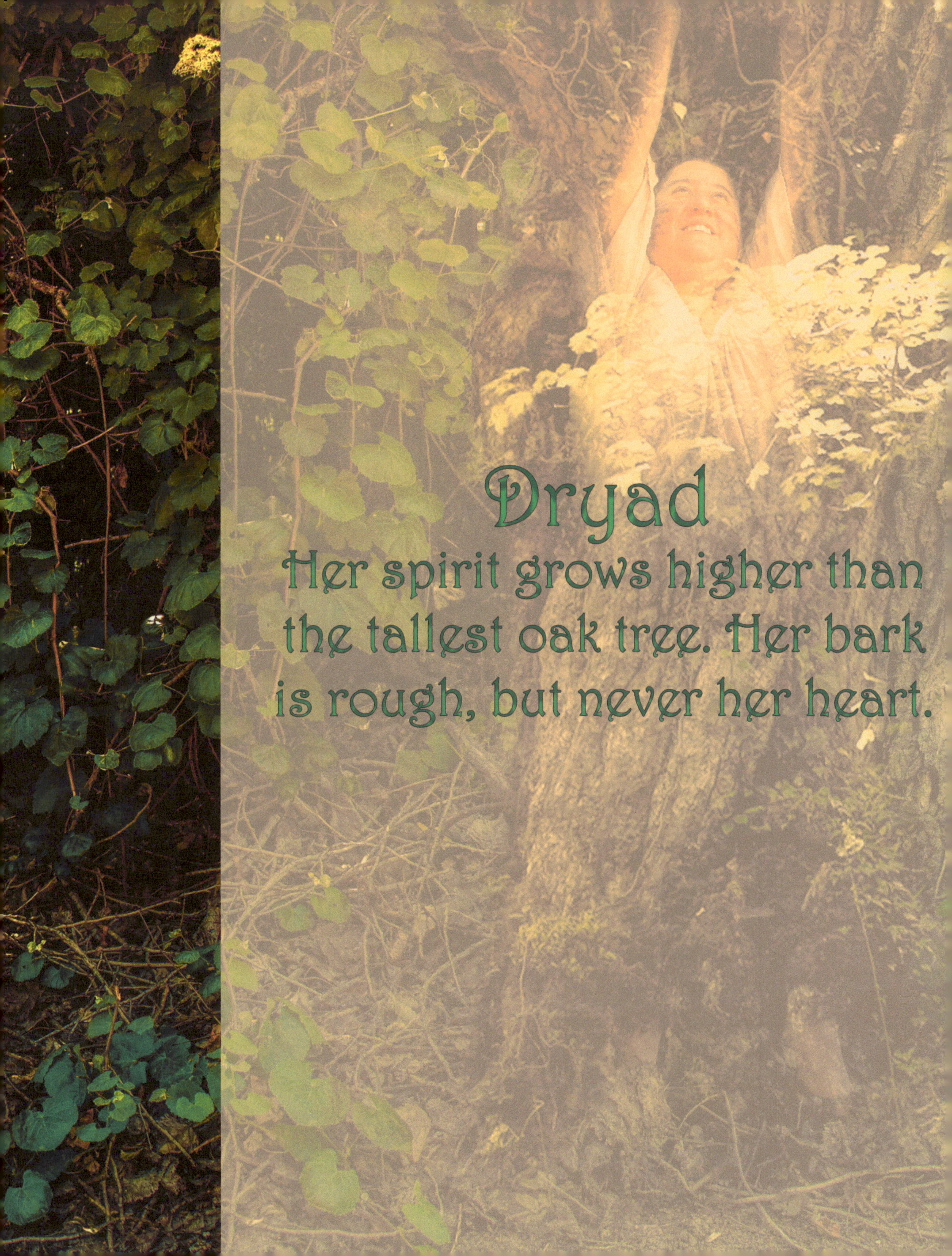
Dryad
Her spirit grows higher than
the tallest oak tree. Her bark
is rough, but never her heart.

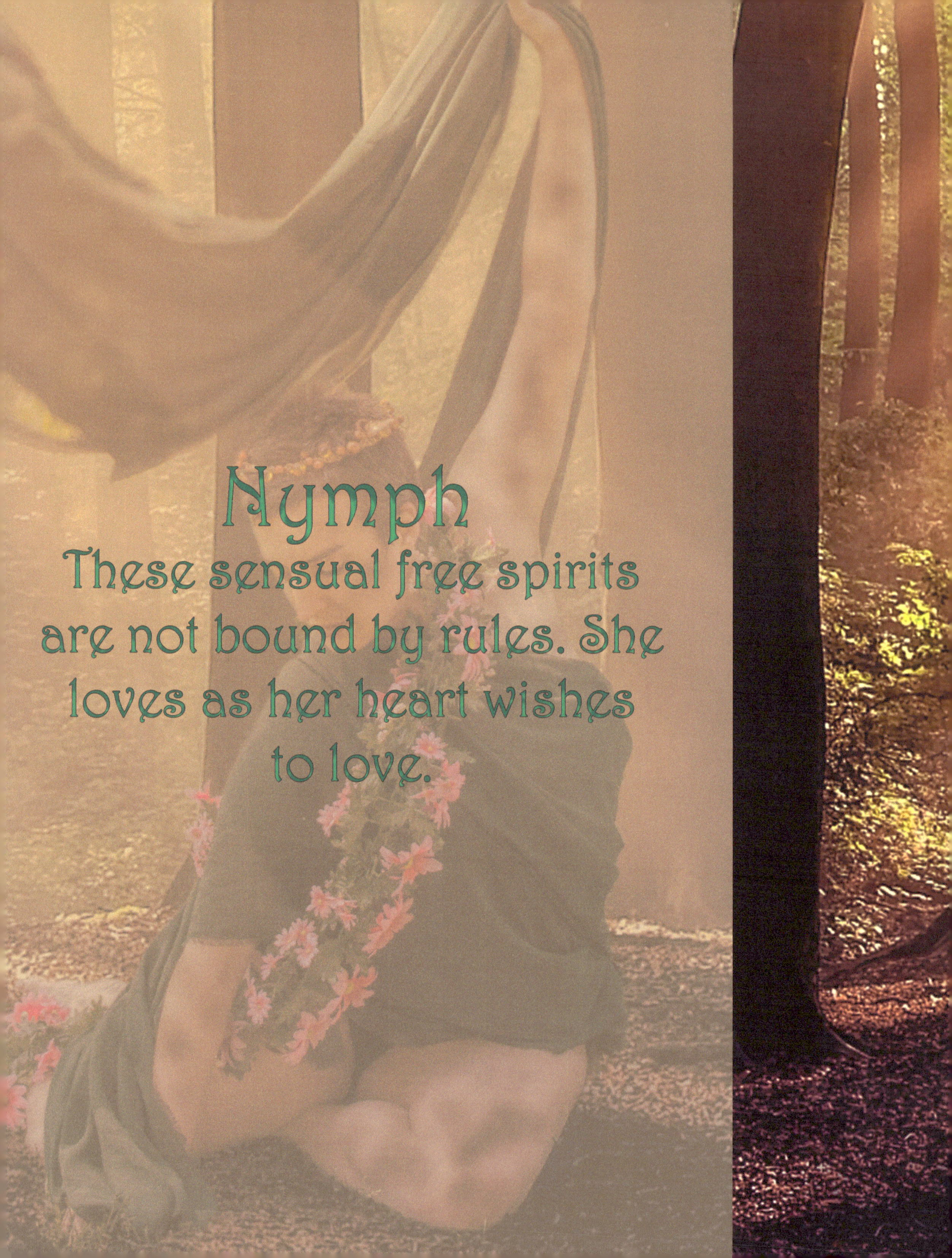
Nymph
These sensual free spirits
are not bound by rules. She
loves as her heart wishes
to love.

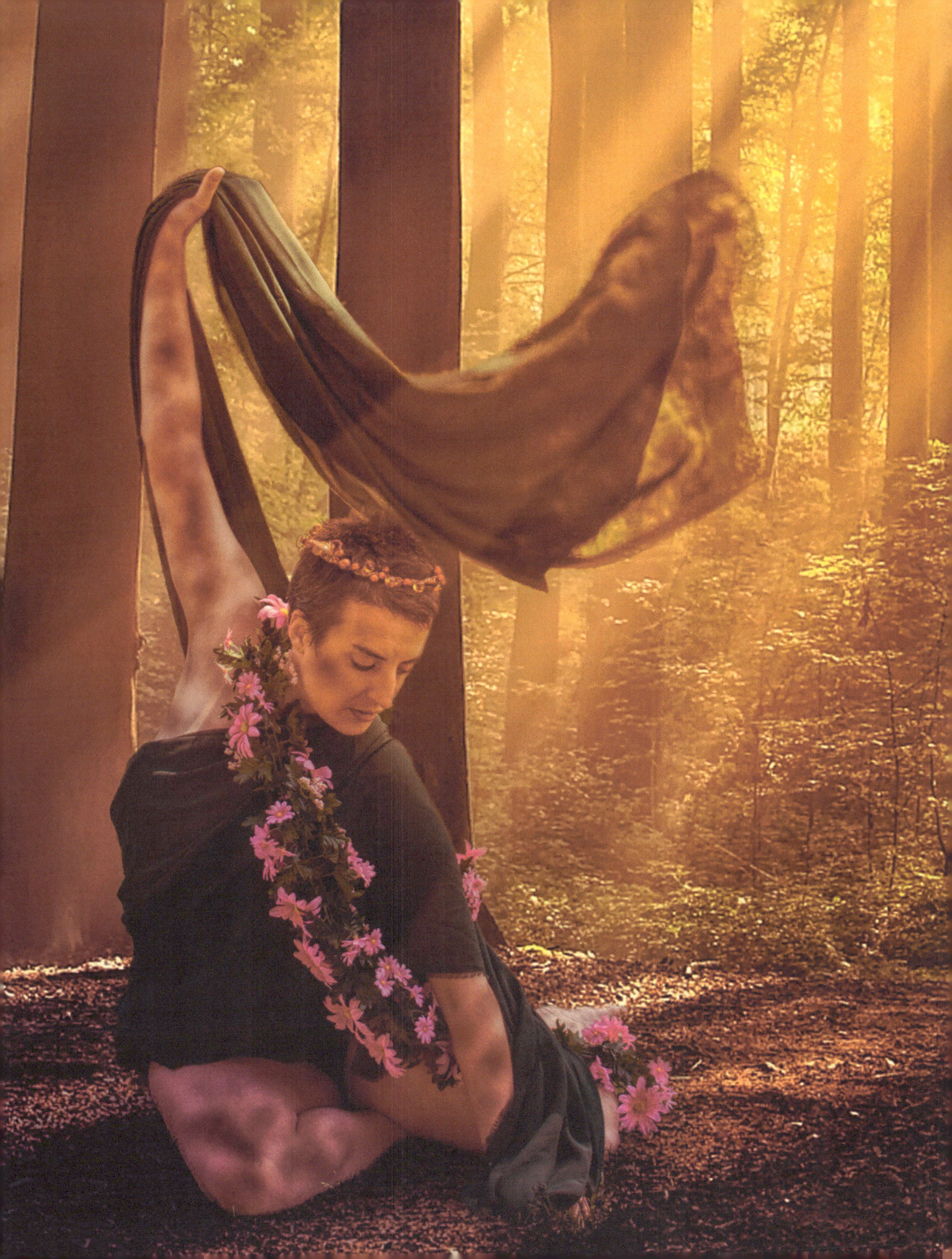

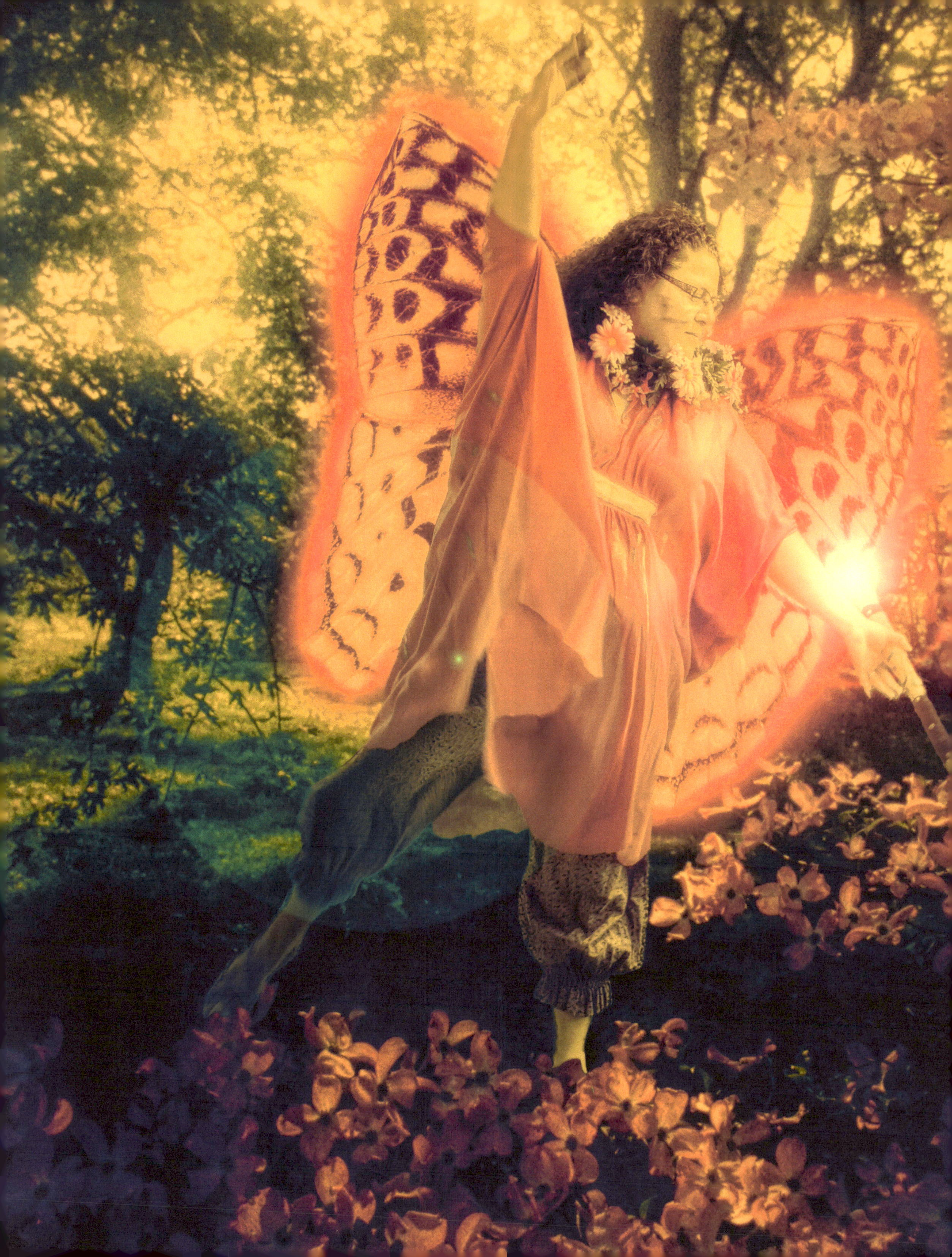

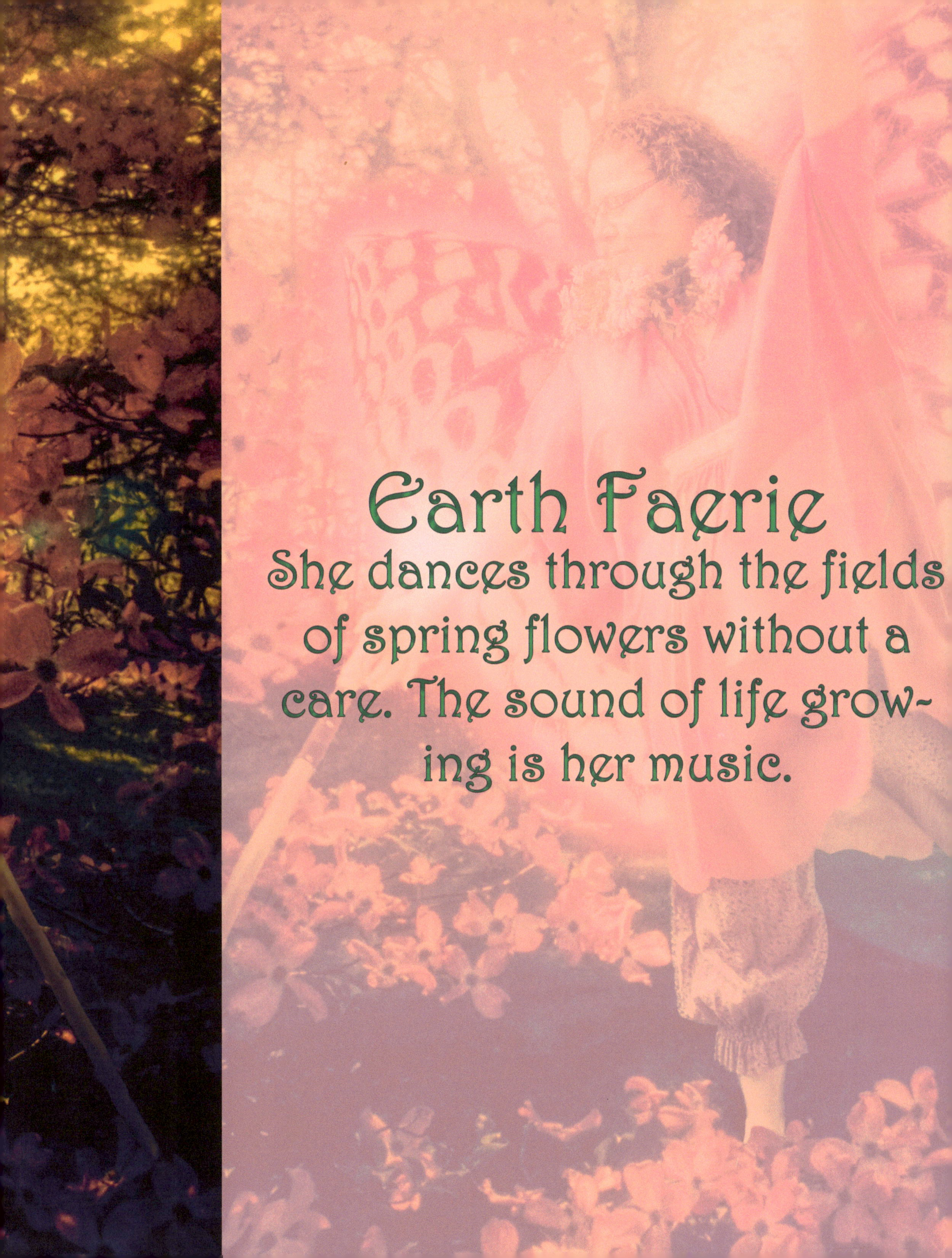
Earth Faerie
She dances through the fields
of spring flowers without a
care. The sound of life grow-
ing is her music.

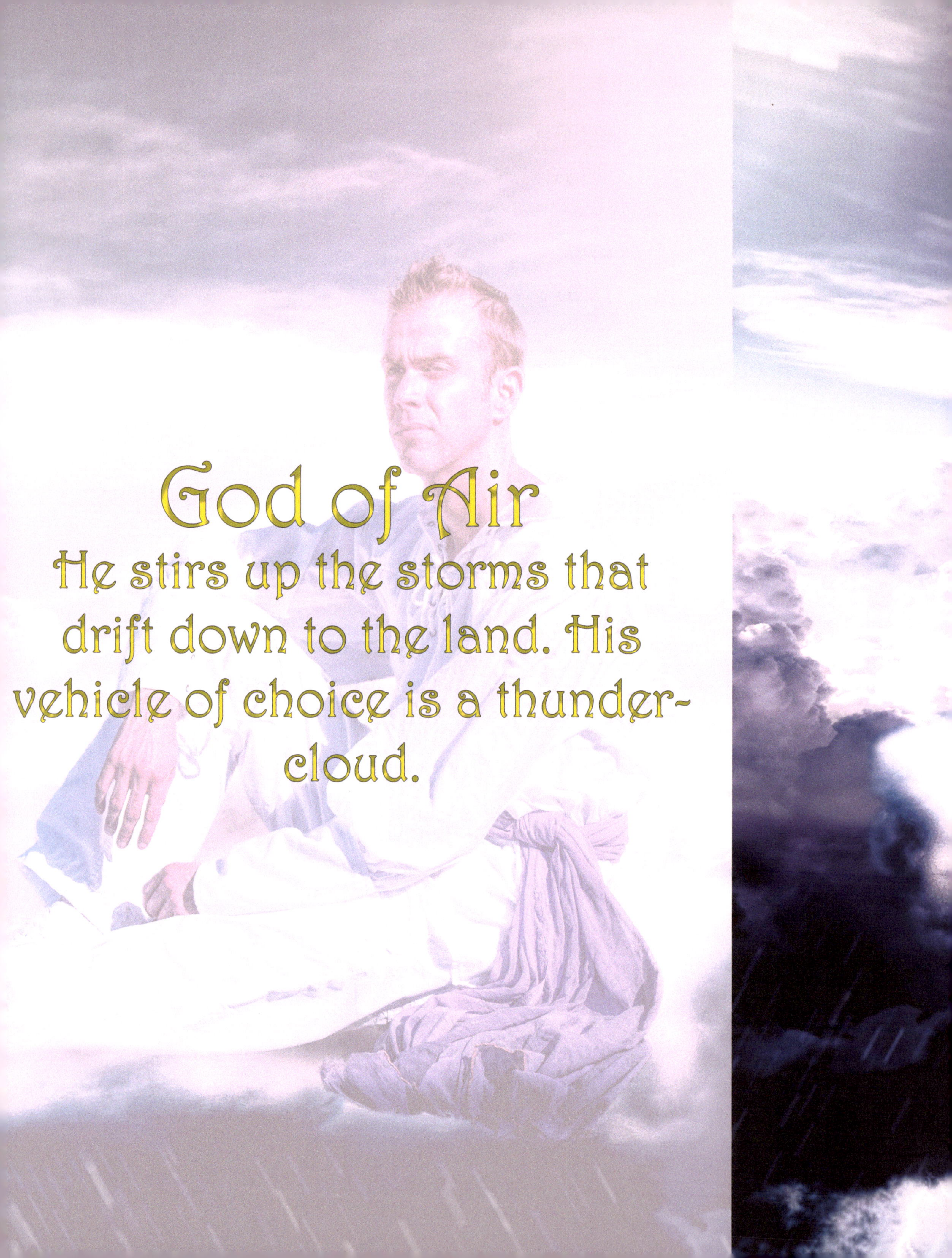

God of Air
He stirs up the storms that drift down to the land. His vehicle of choice is a thunder-cloud.

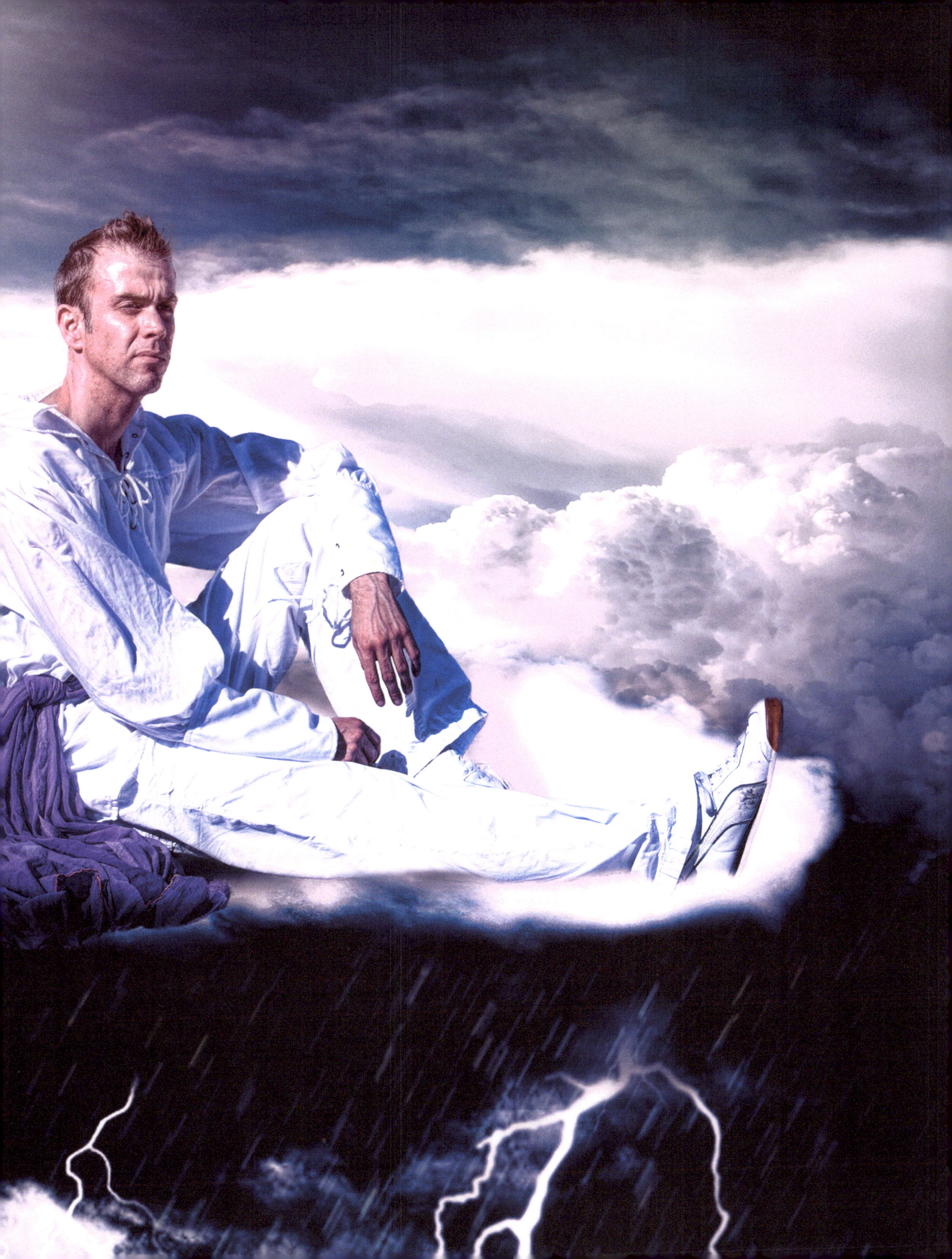

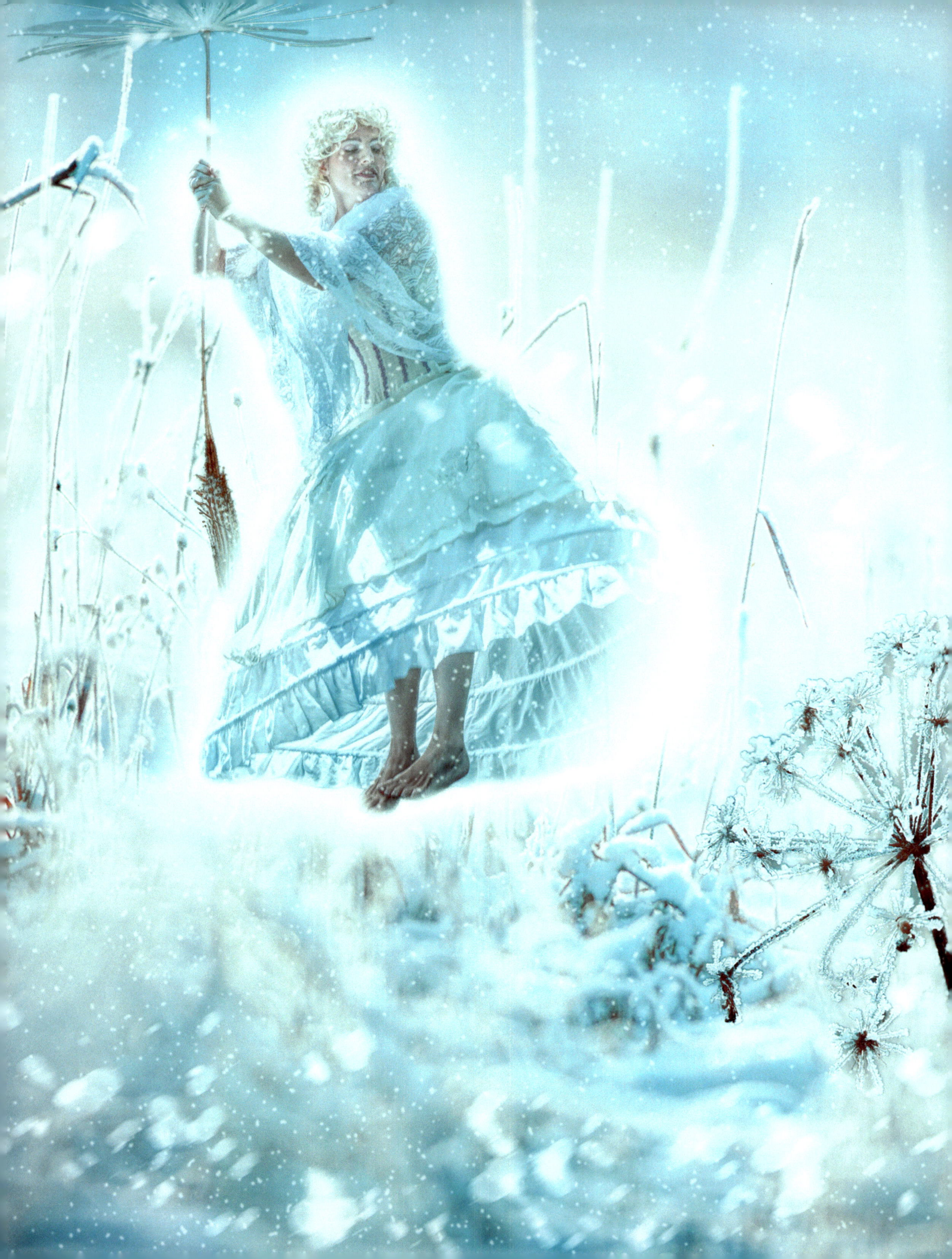

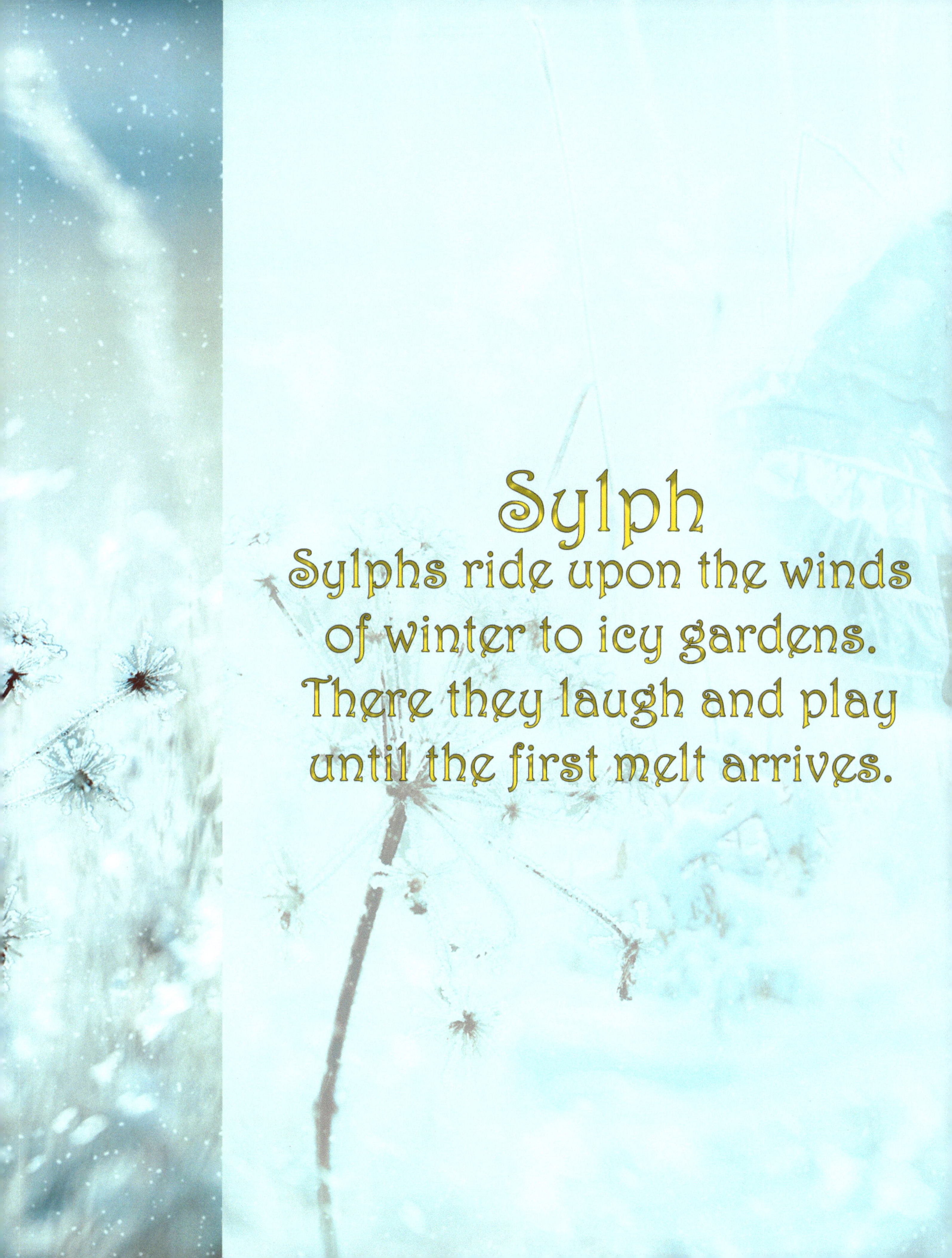
Sylph
Sylphs ride upon the winds
of winter to icy gardens.
There they laugh and play
until the first melt arrives.

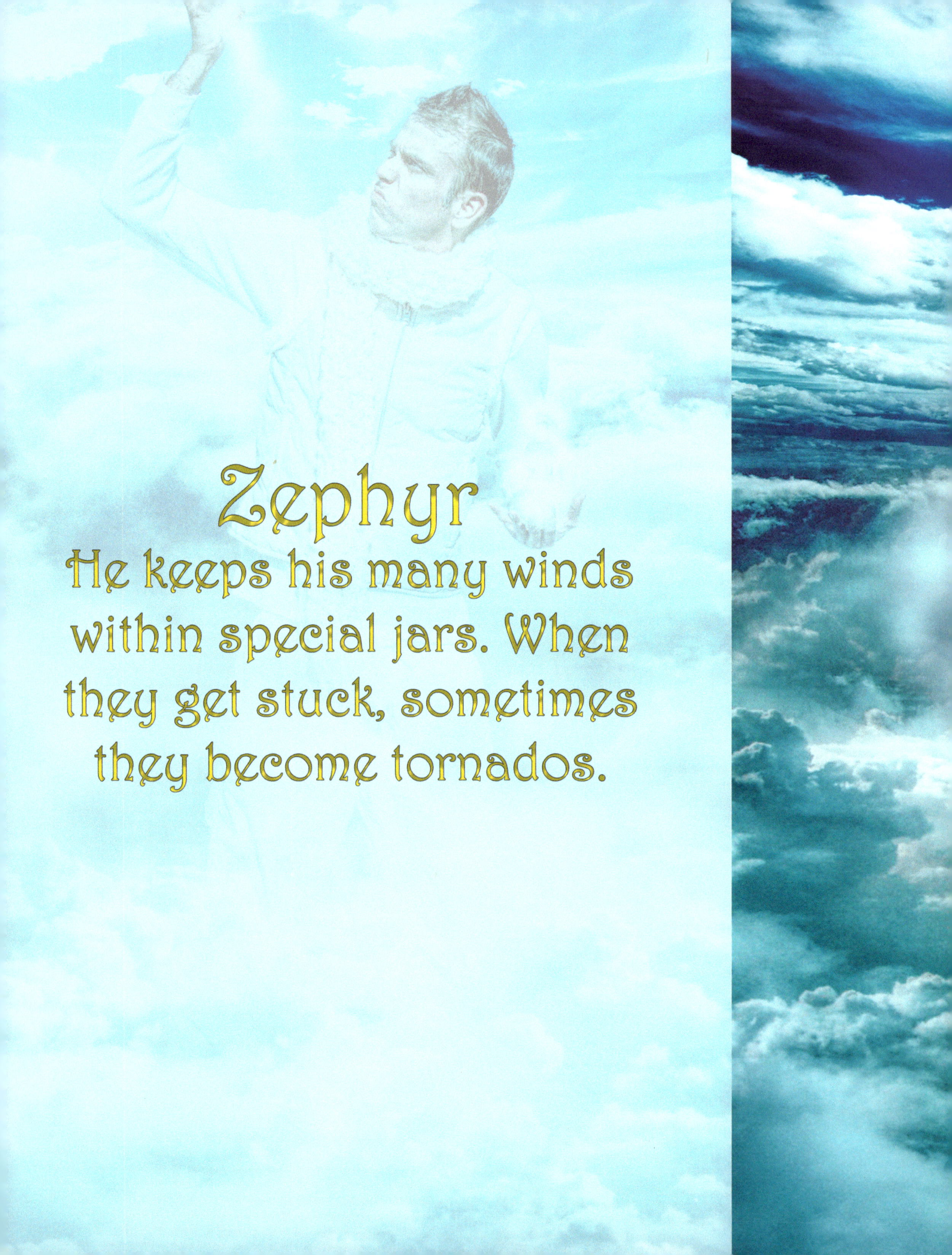

Zephyr
He keeps his many winds
within special jars. When
they get stuck, sometimes
they become tornados.

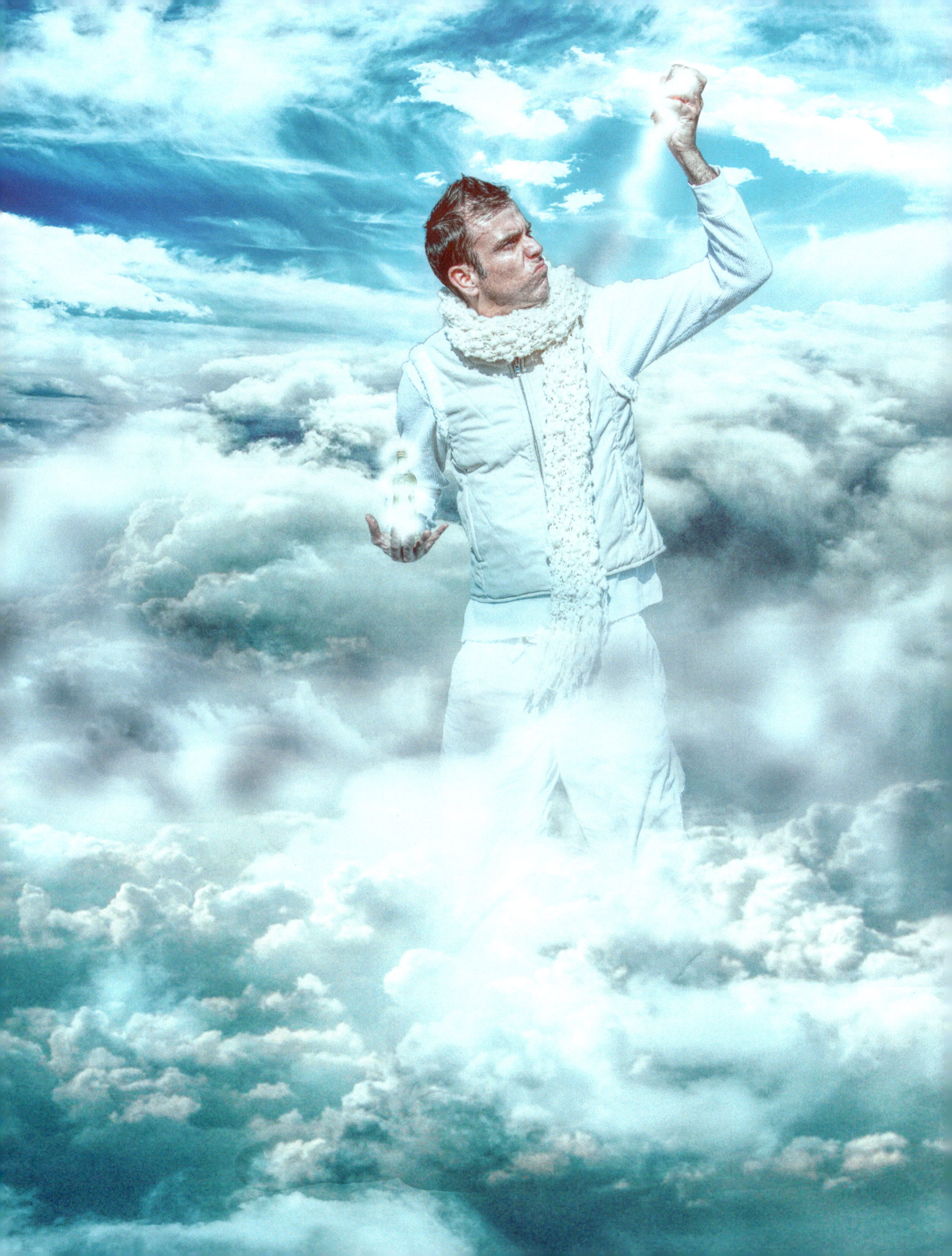

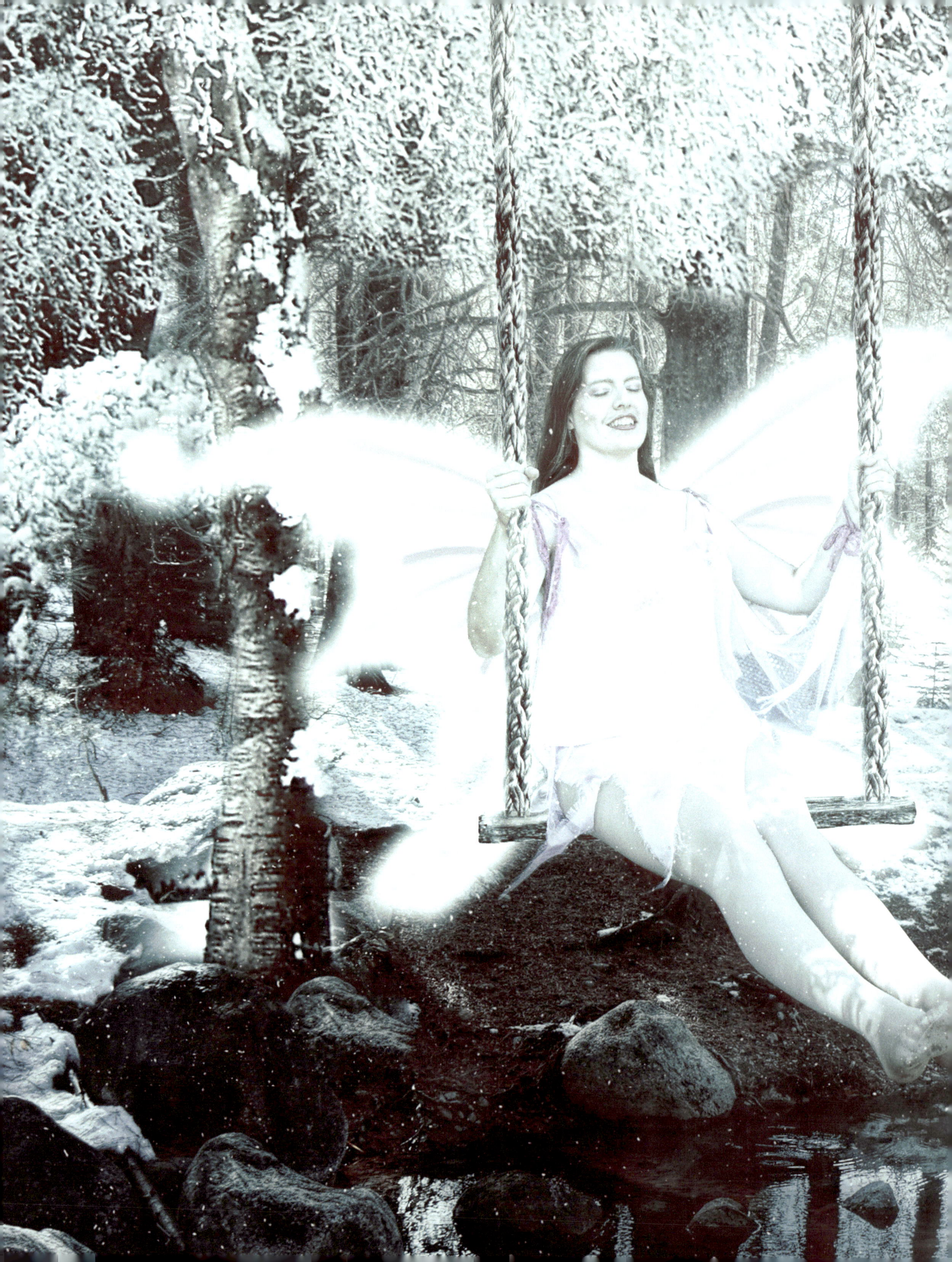

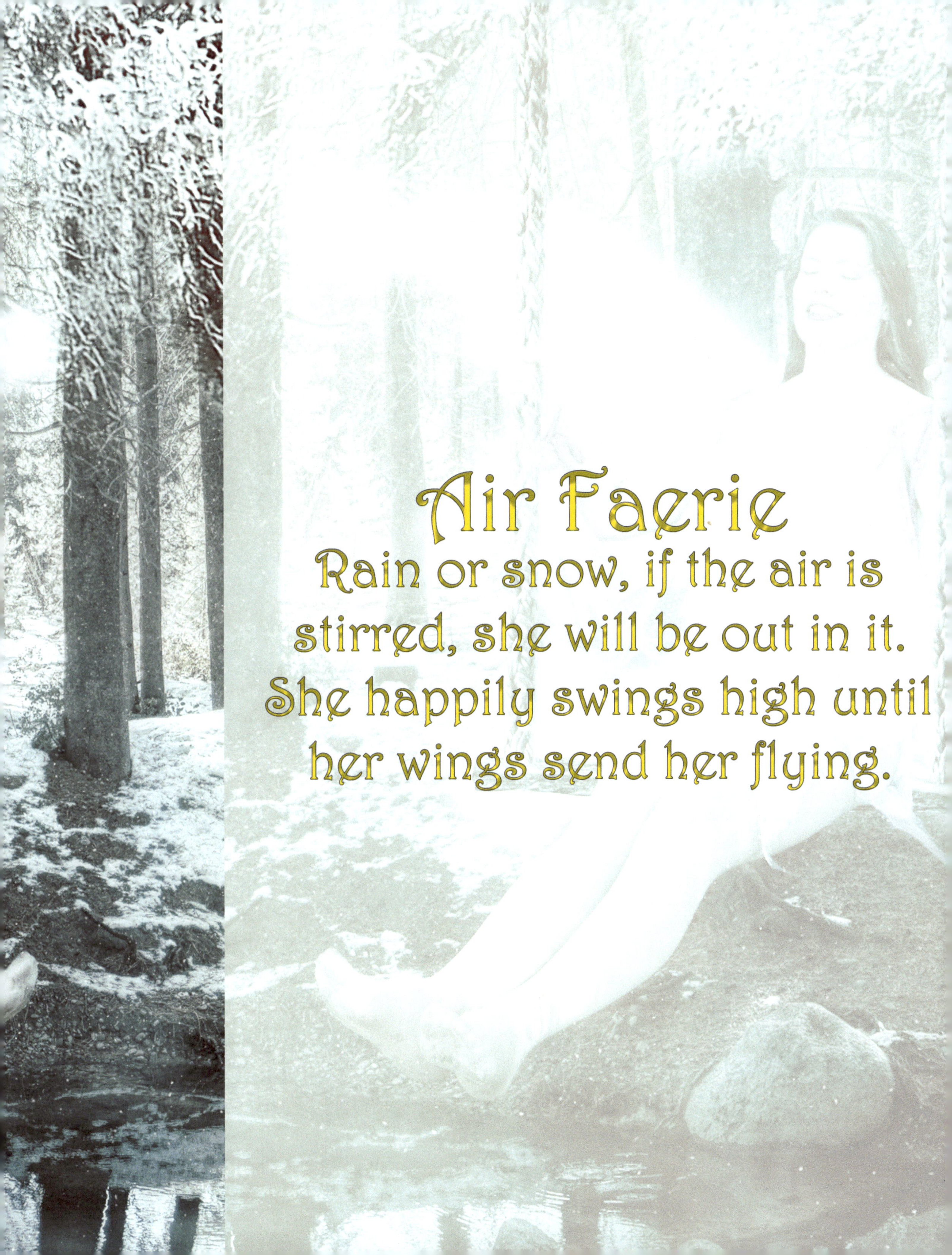

Air Faerie
Rain or snow, if the air is
stirred, she will be out in it.
She happily swings high until
her wings send her flying.

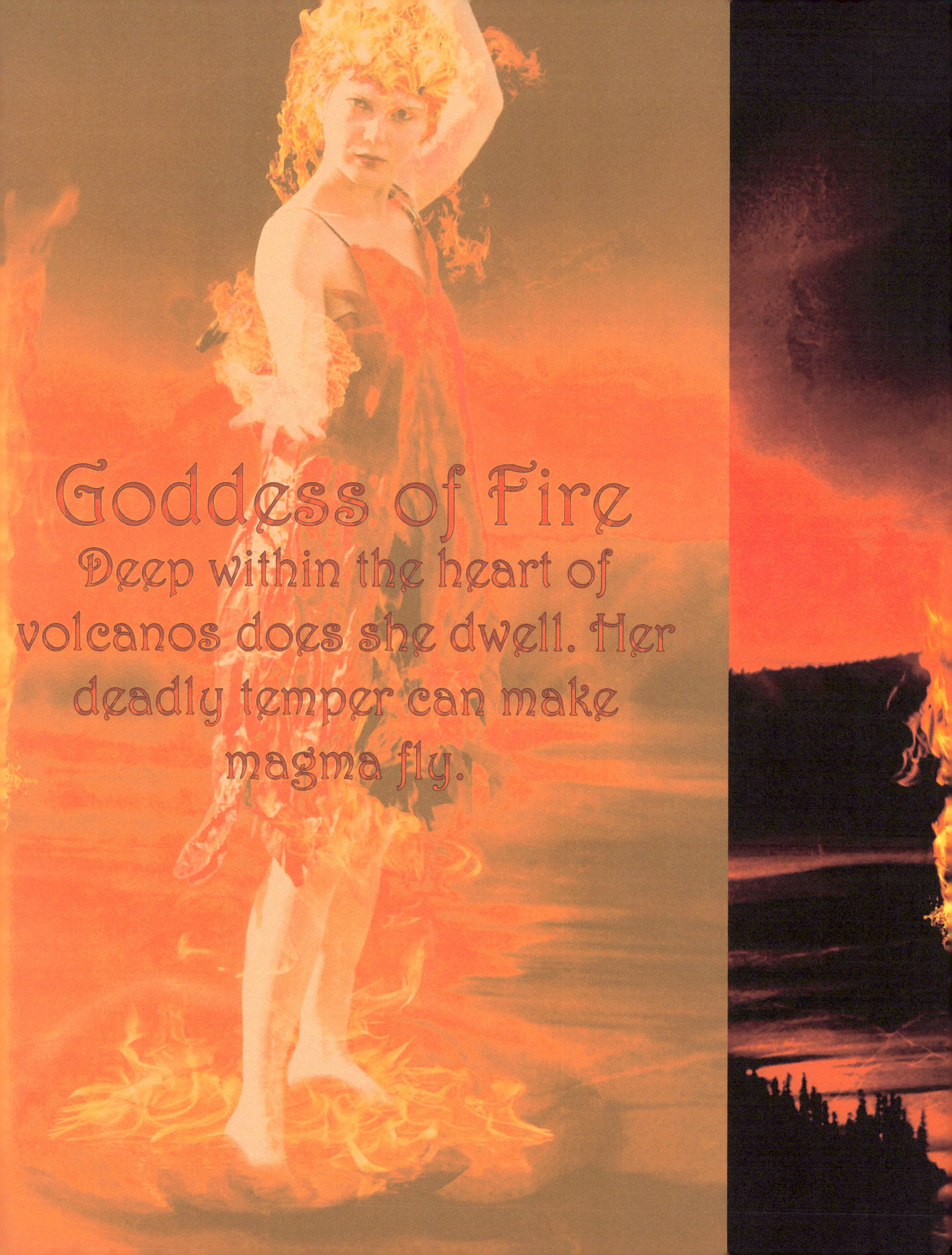
Goddess of Fire
Deep within the heart of volcanos does she dwell. Her deadly temper can make magma fly.

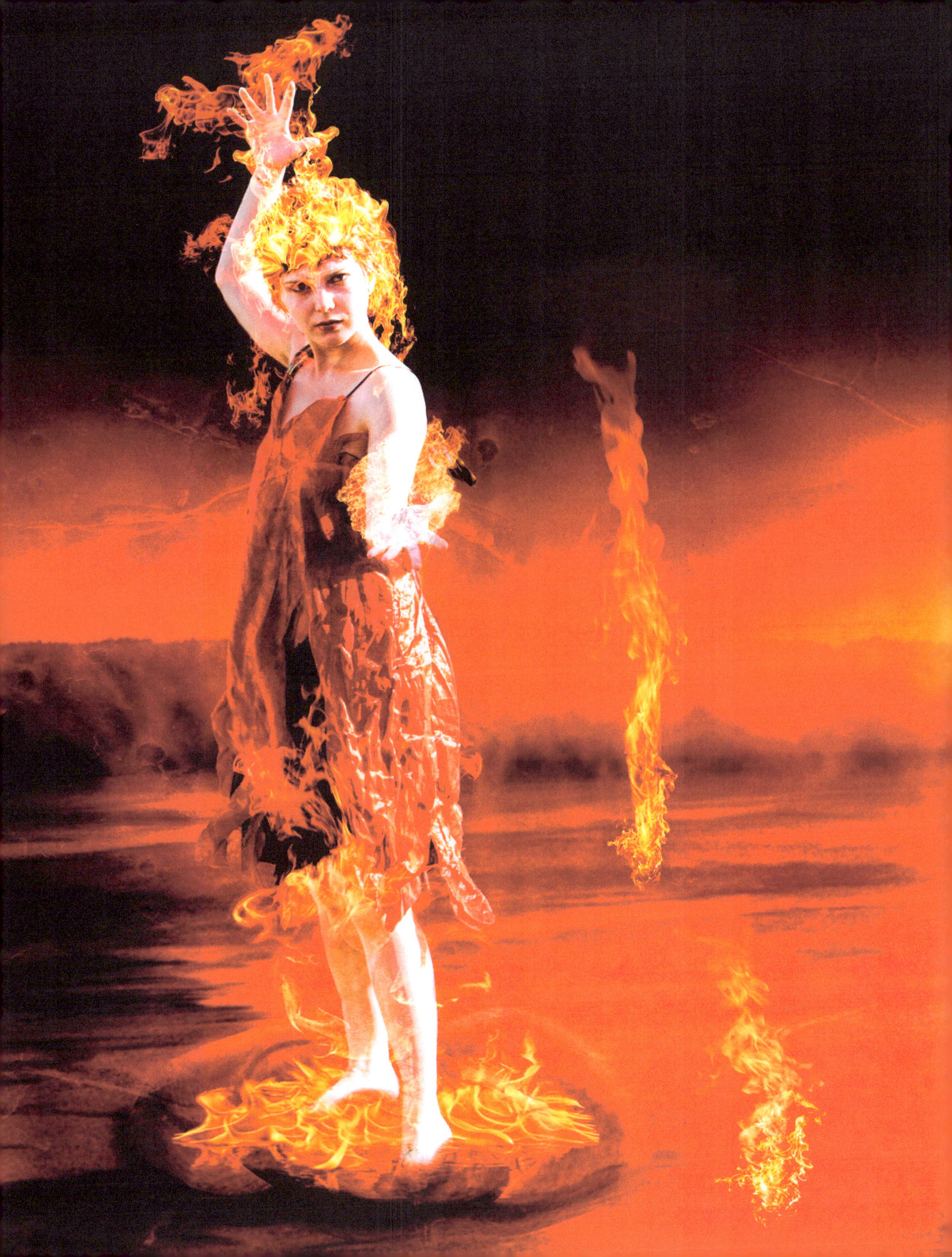

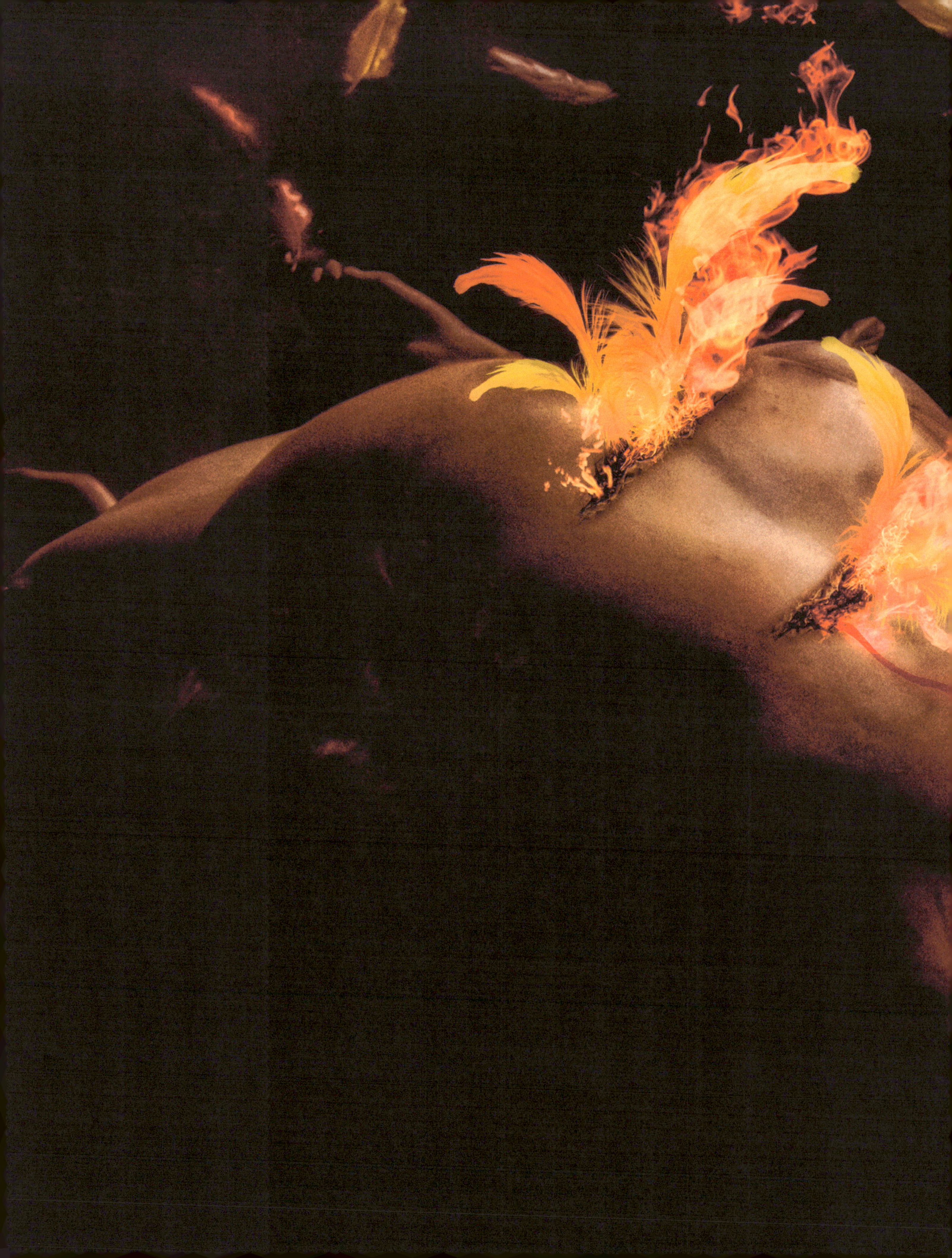

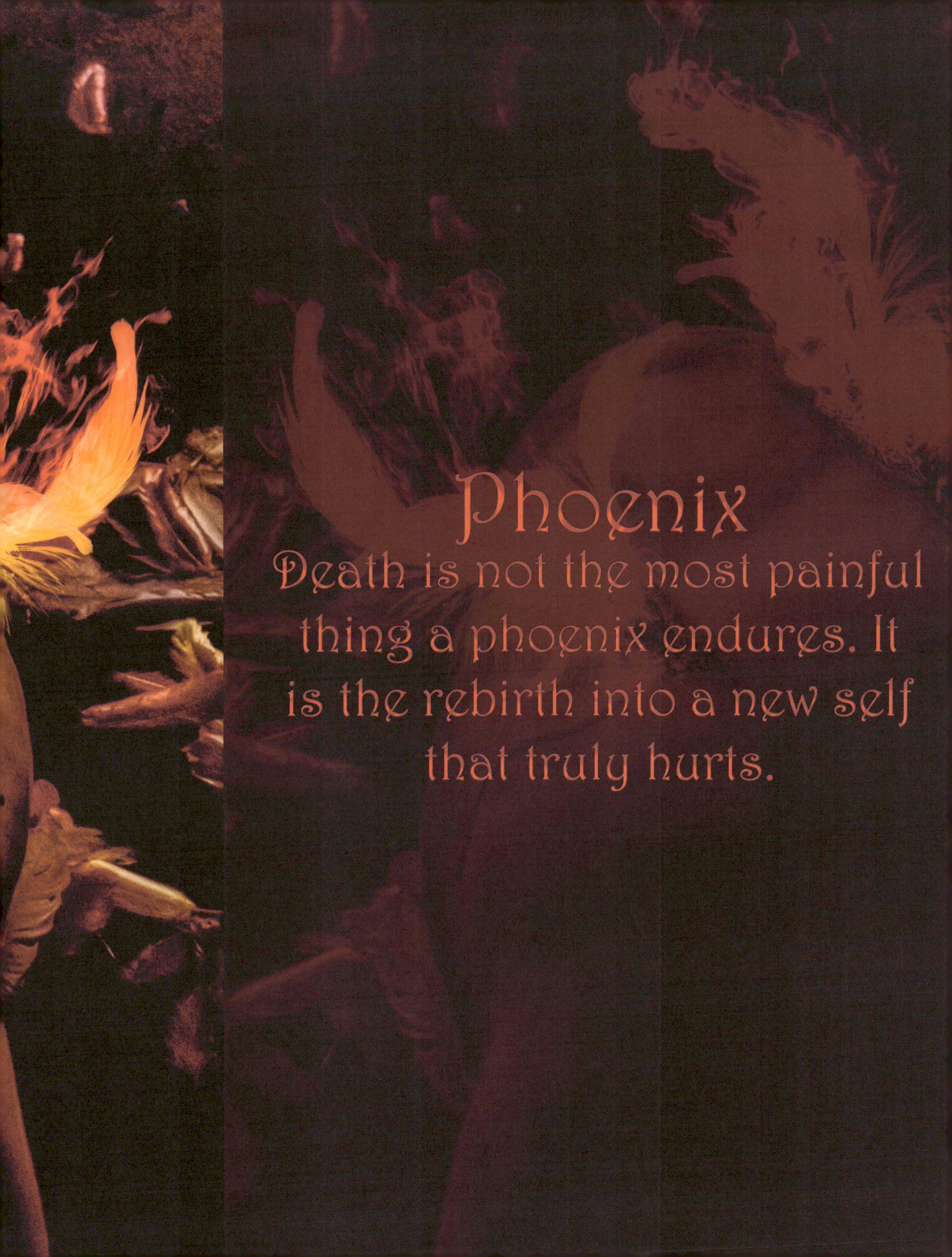

Phoenix
Death is not the most painful
thing a phoenix endures. It
is the rebirth into a new self
that truly hurts.

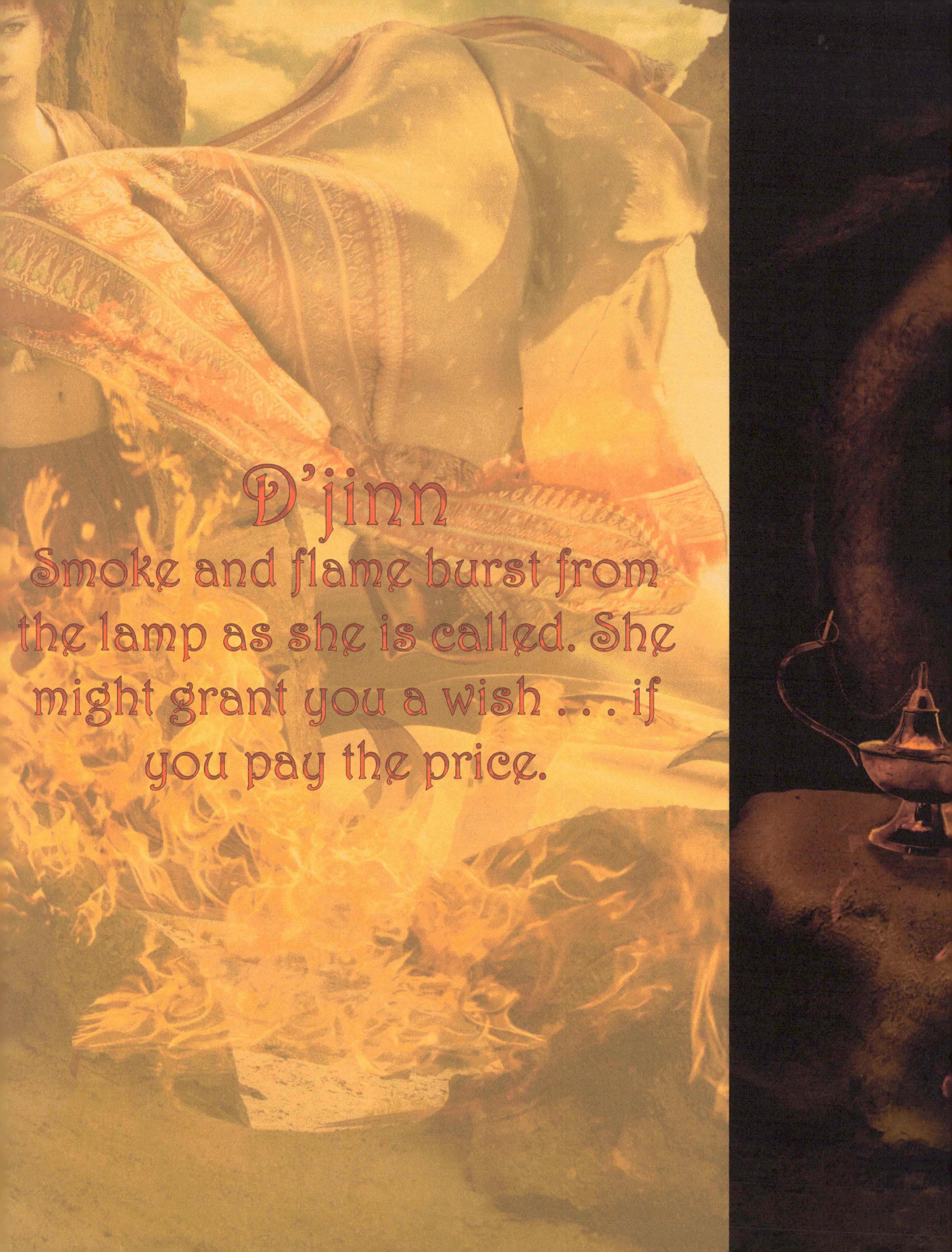

D'jinn
Smoke and flame burst from
the lamp as she is called. She
might grant you a wish . . . if
you pay the price.

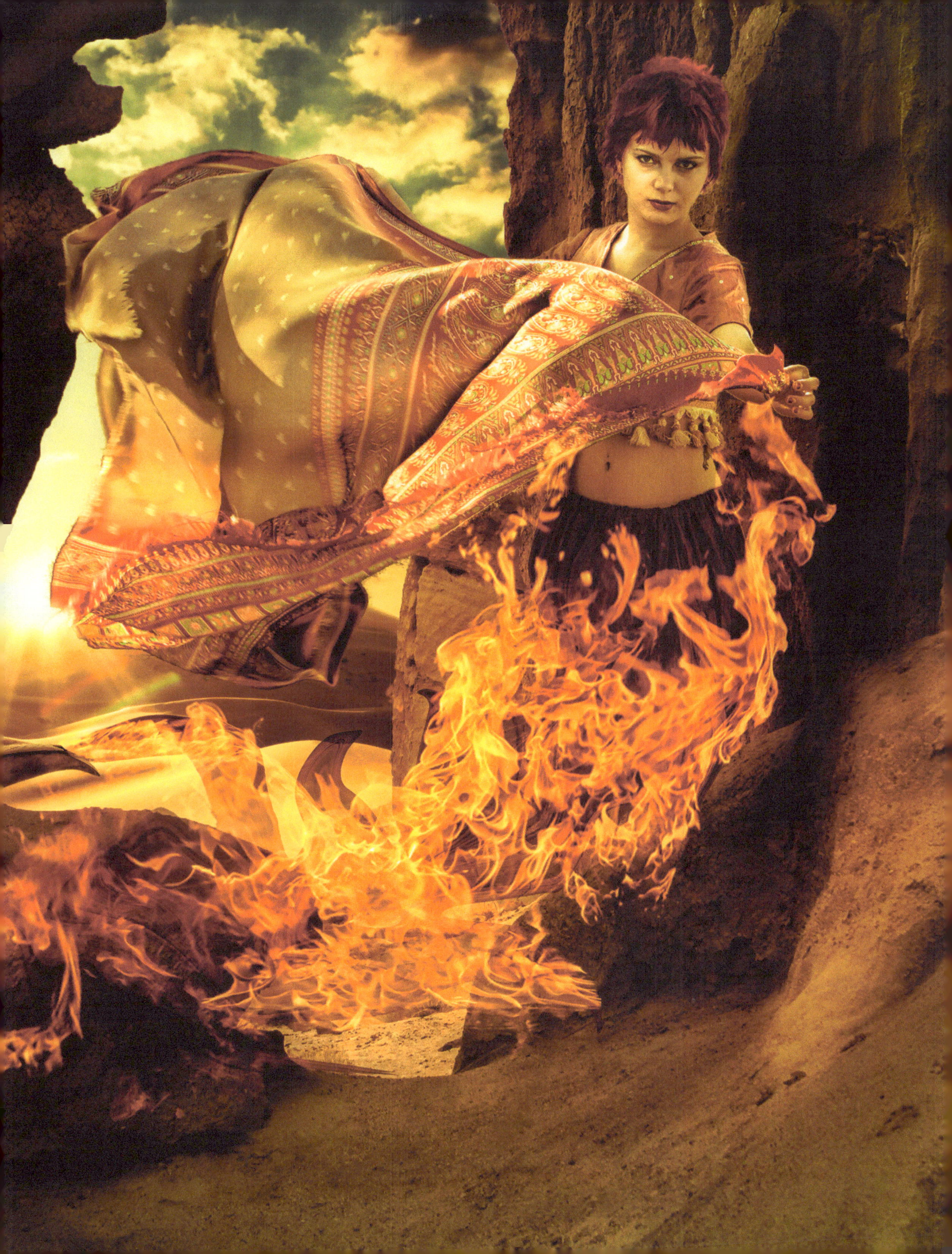

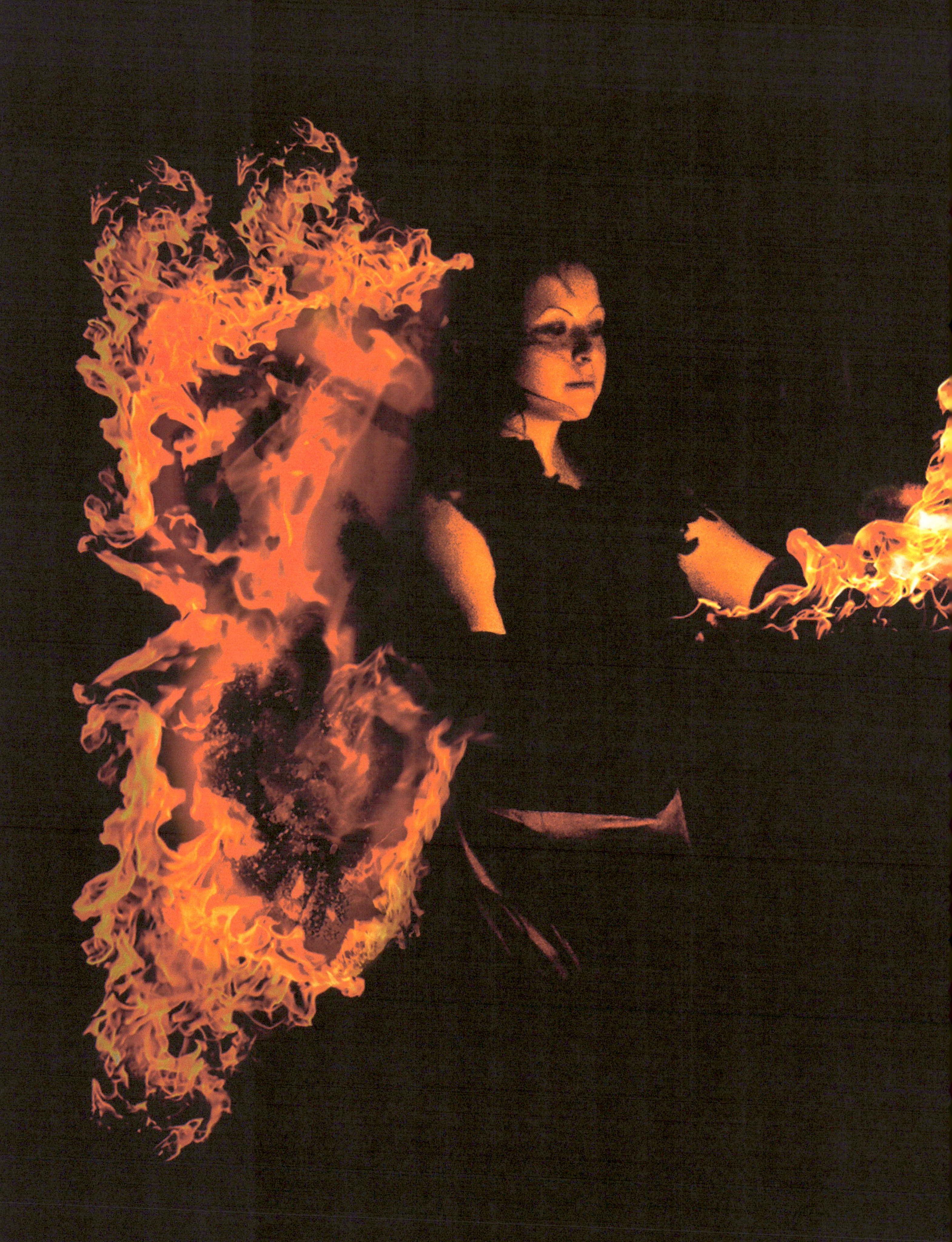

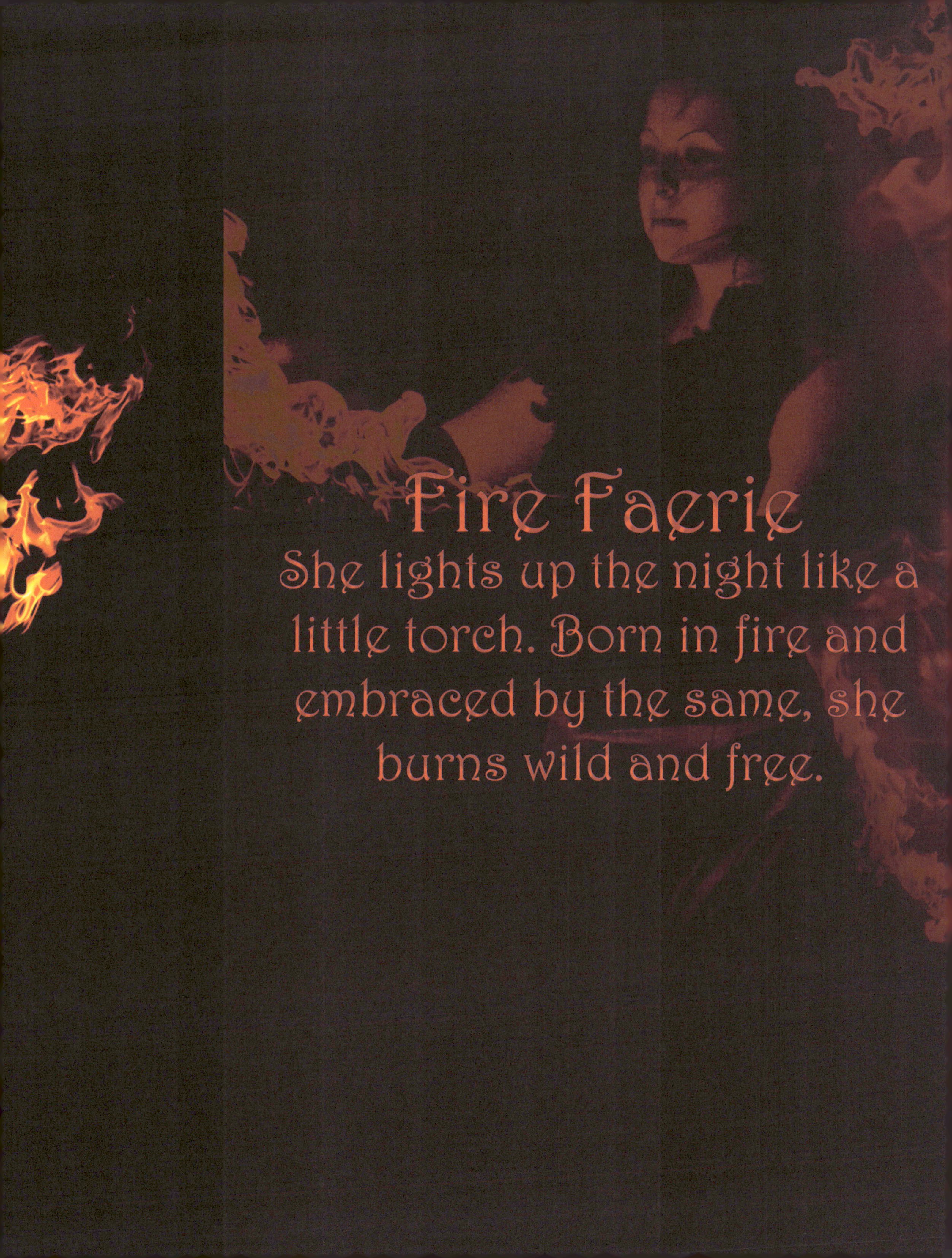

Fire Faerie

She lights up the night like a little torch. Born in fire and embraced by the same, she burns wild and free.

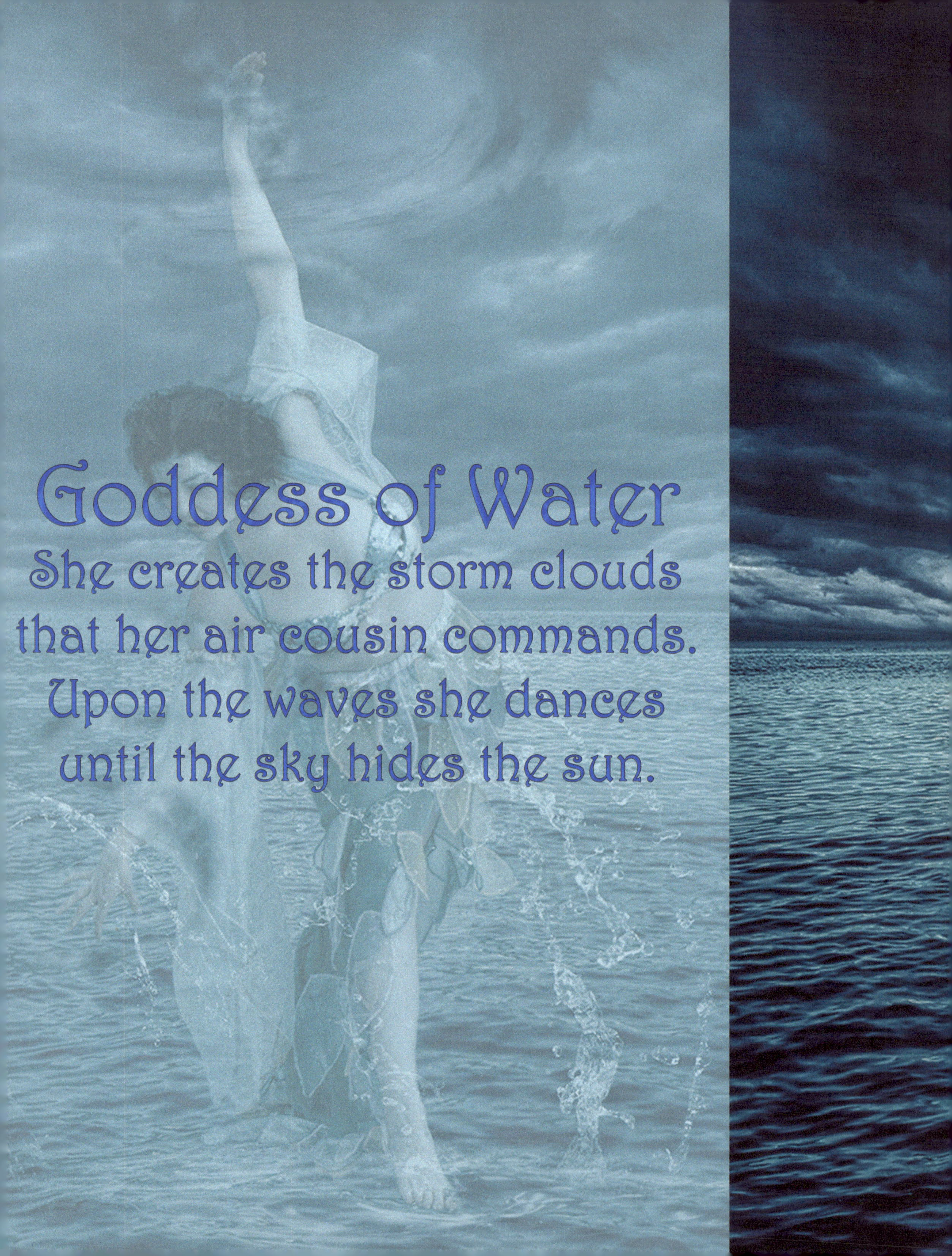

Goddess of Water
She creates the storm clouds
that her air cousin commands.
Upon the waves she dances
until the sky hides the sun.

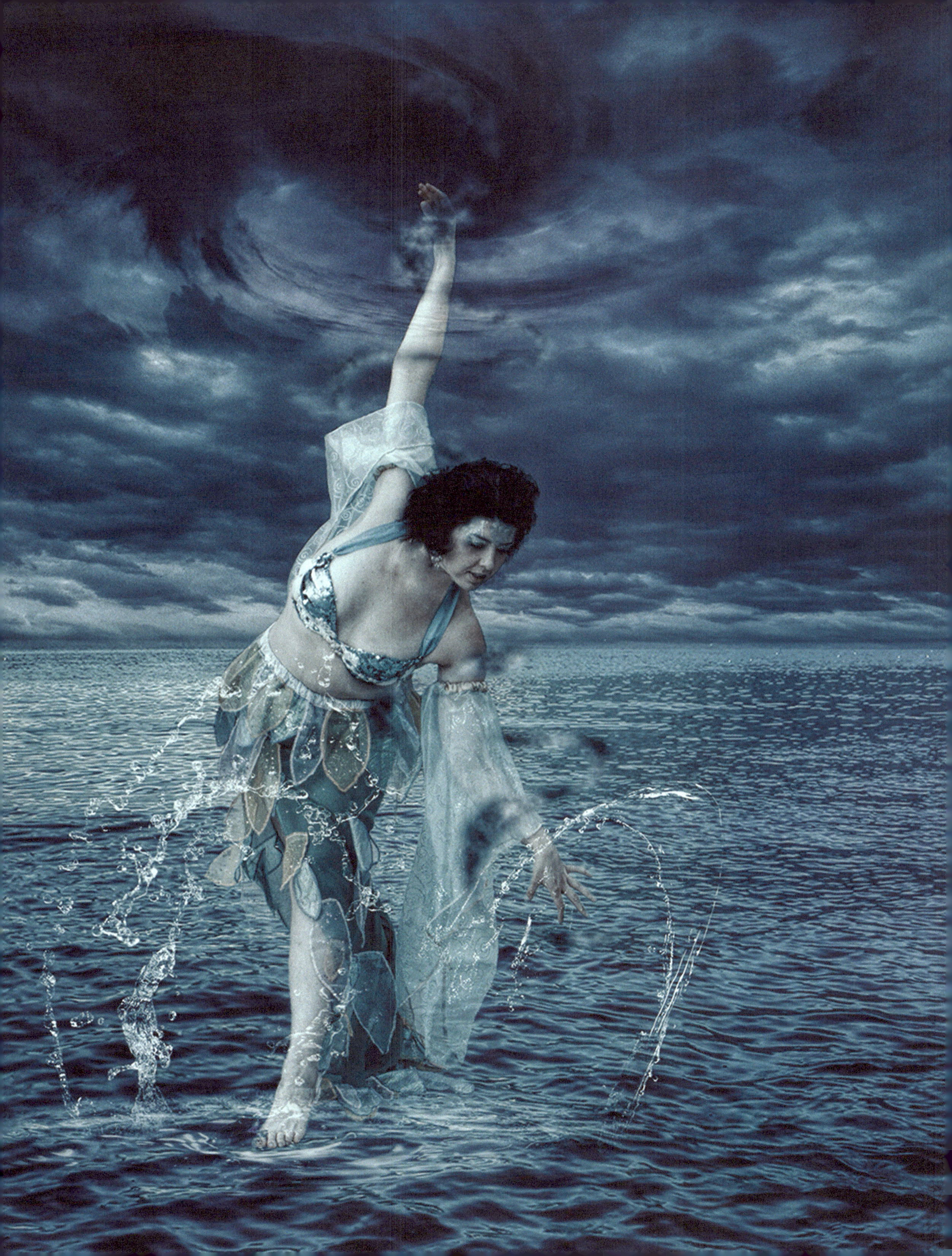

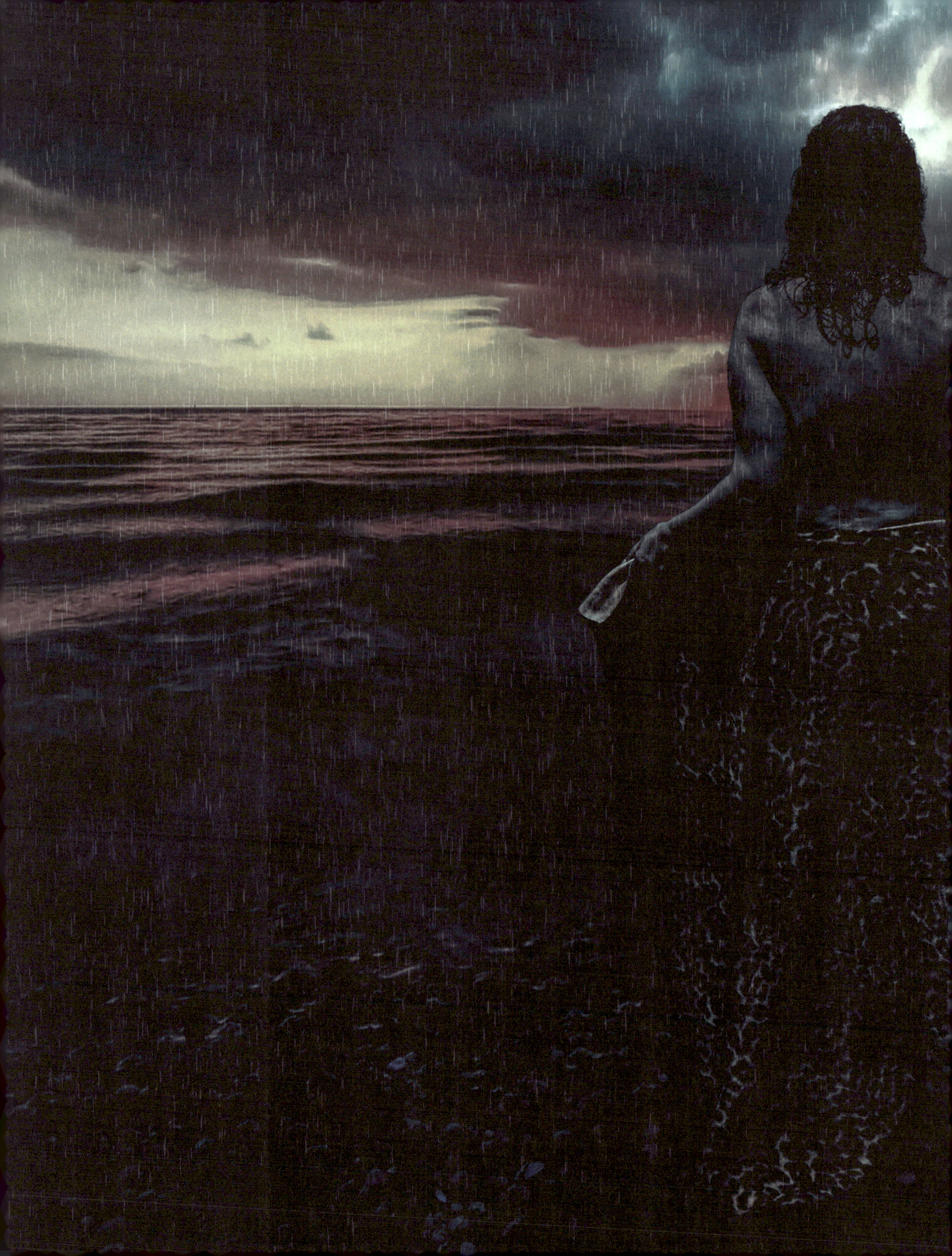

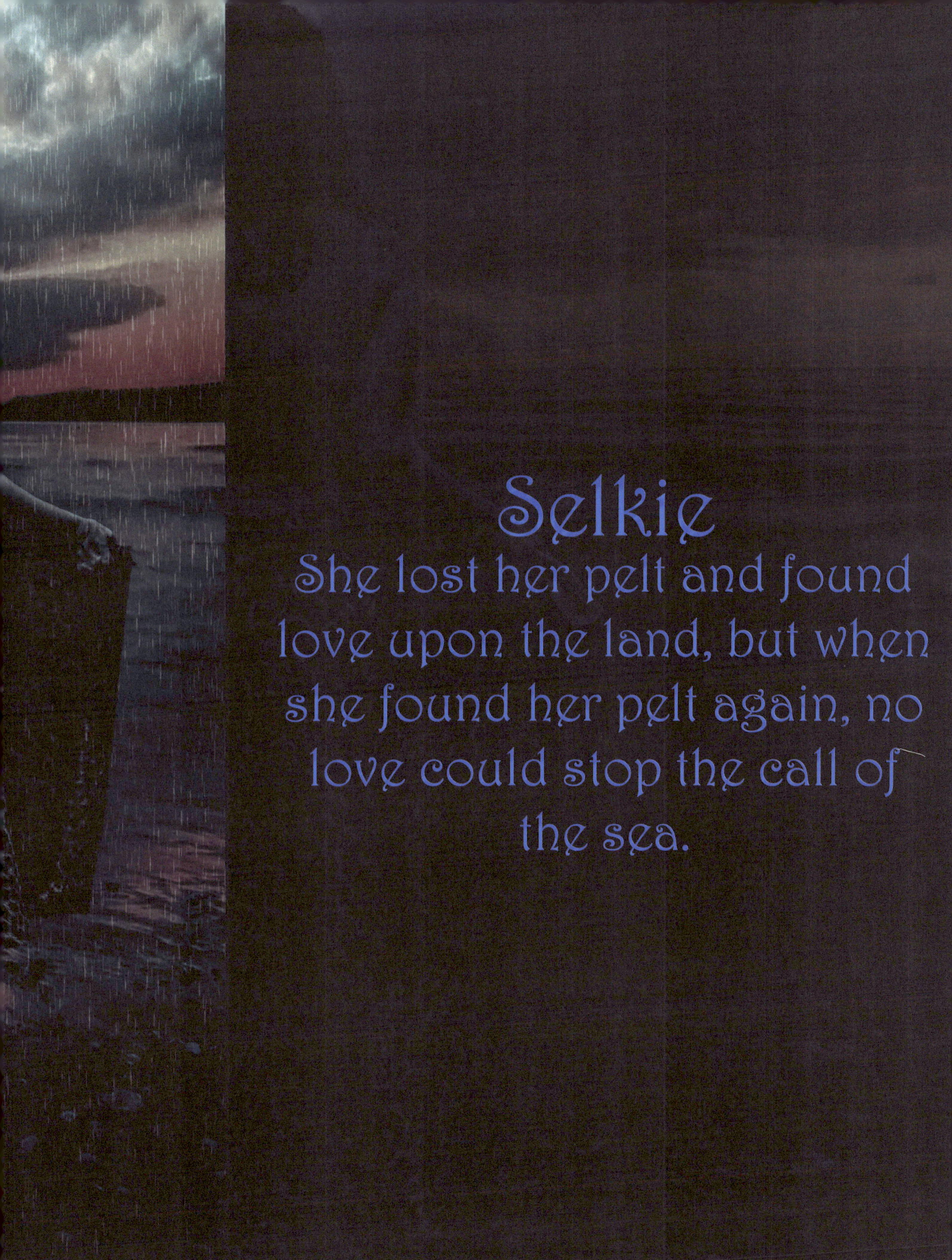

Selkie
She lost her pelt and found love upon the land, but when she found her pelt again, no love could stop the call of the sea.

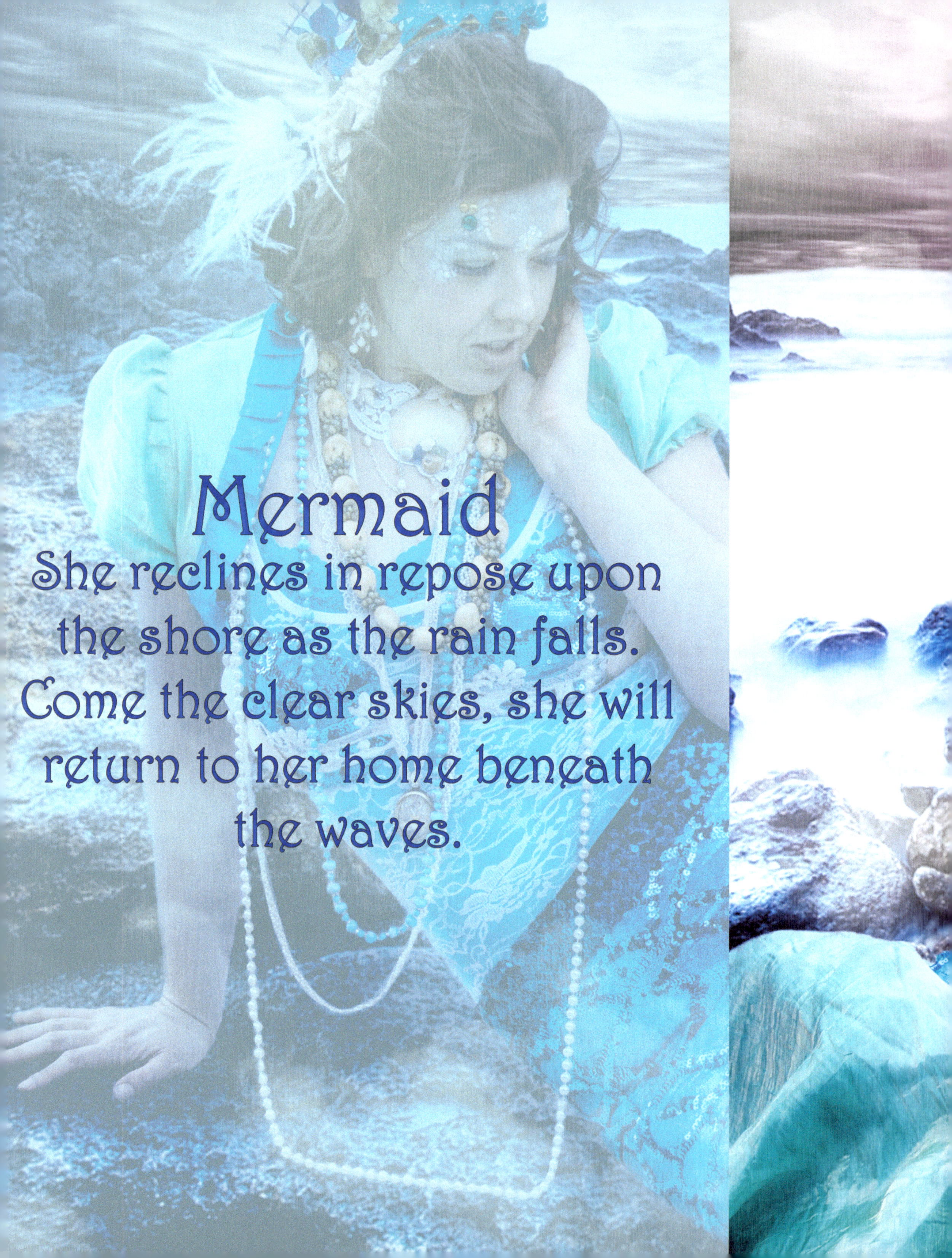

Mermaid
She reclines in repose upon
the shore as the rain falls.
Come the clear skies, she will
return to her home beneath
the waves.

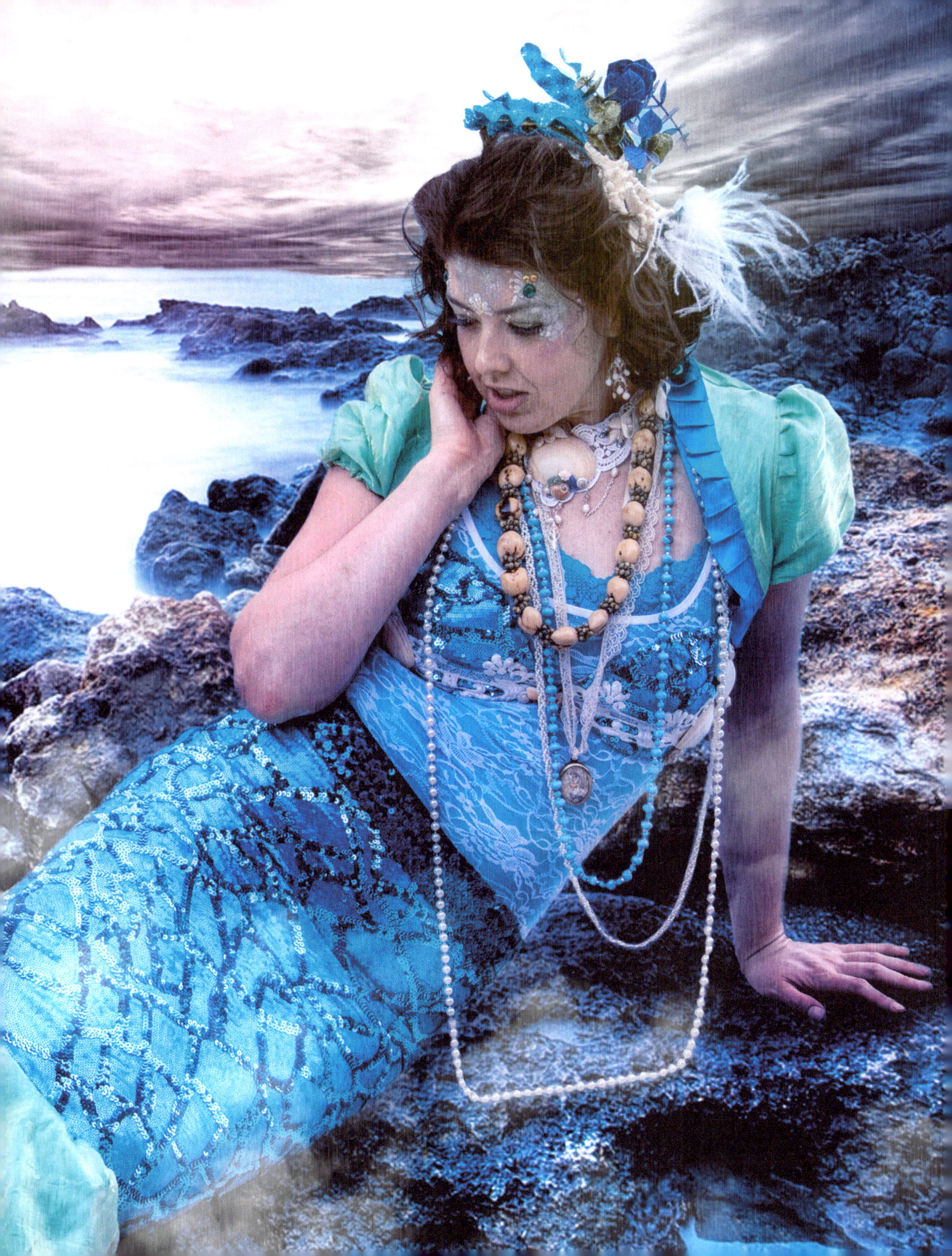

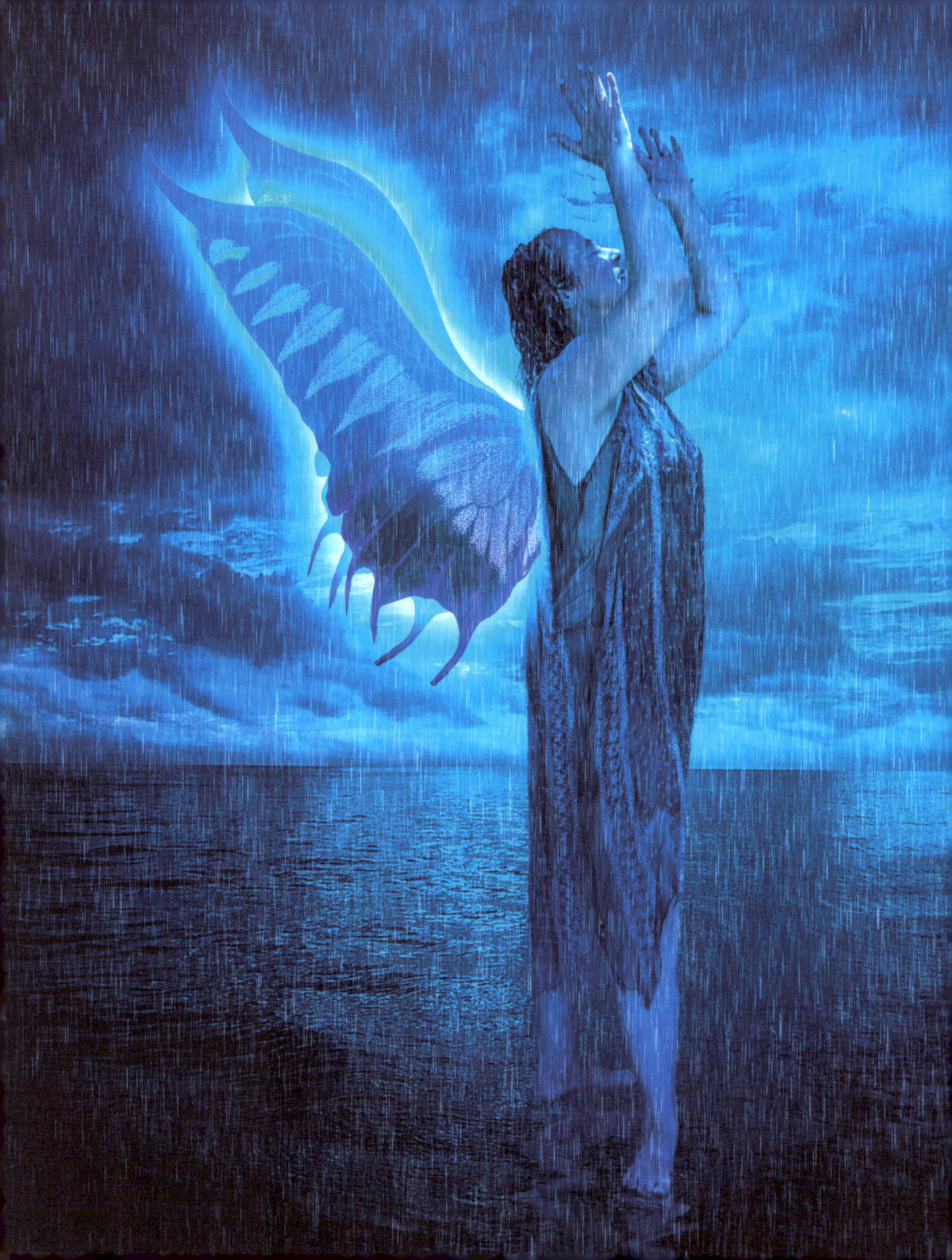

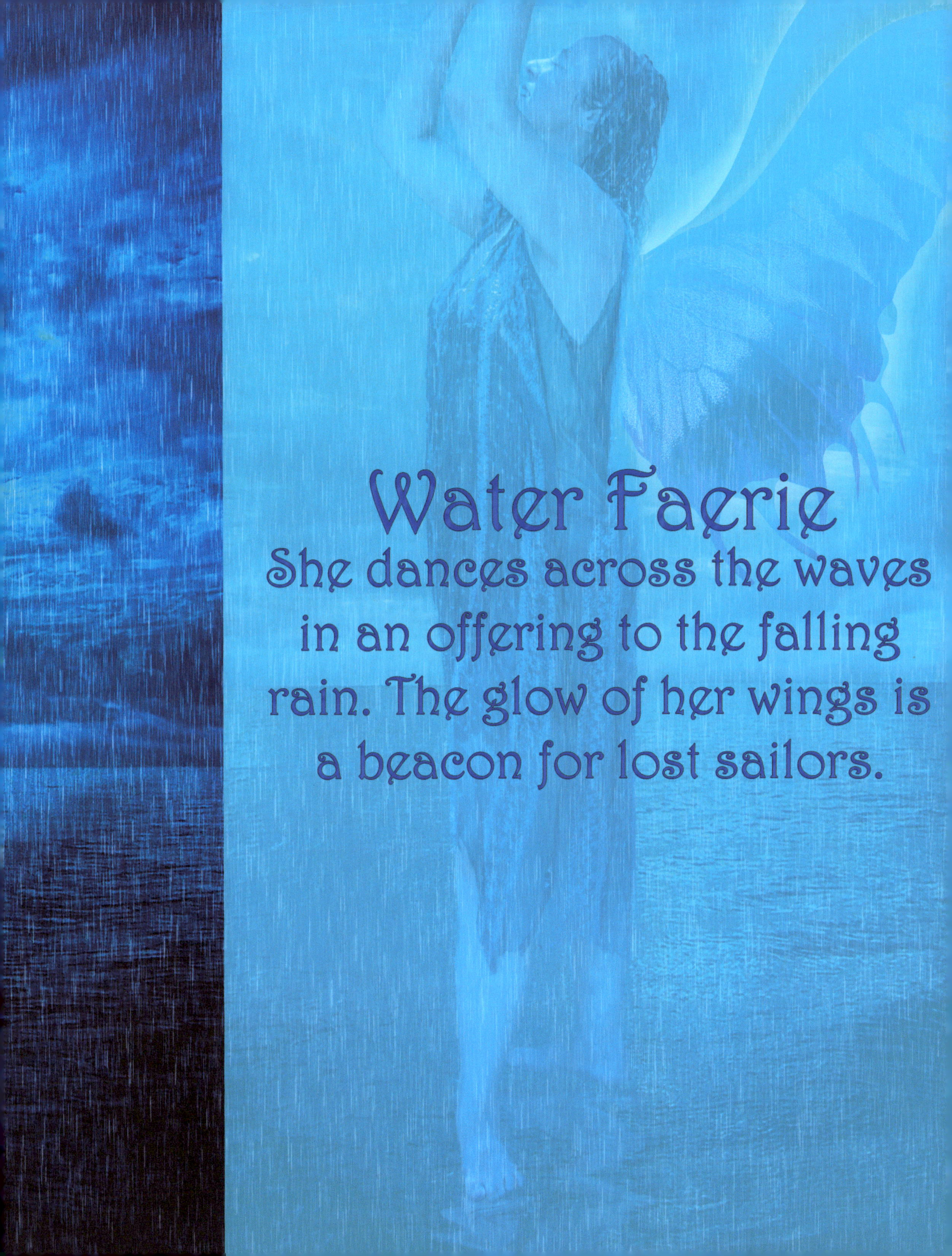
Water Faerie
She dances across the waves
in an offering to the falling
rain. The glow of her wings is
a beacon for lost sailors.

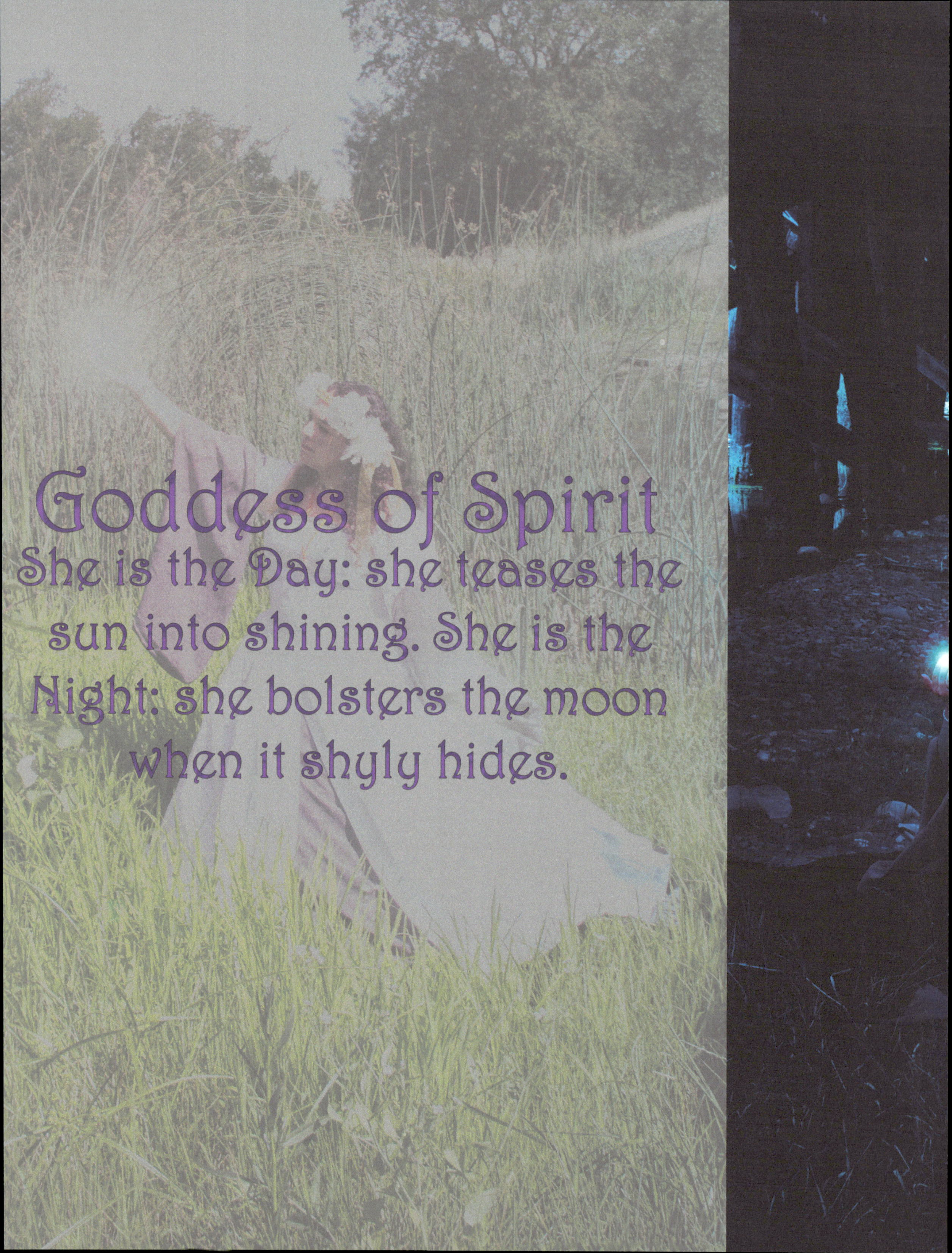

Goddess of Spirit
She is the Day: she teases the
sun into shining. She is the
Night: she bolsters the moon
when it shyly hides.

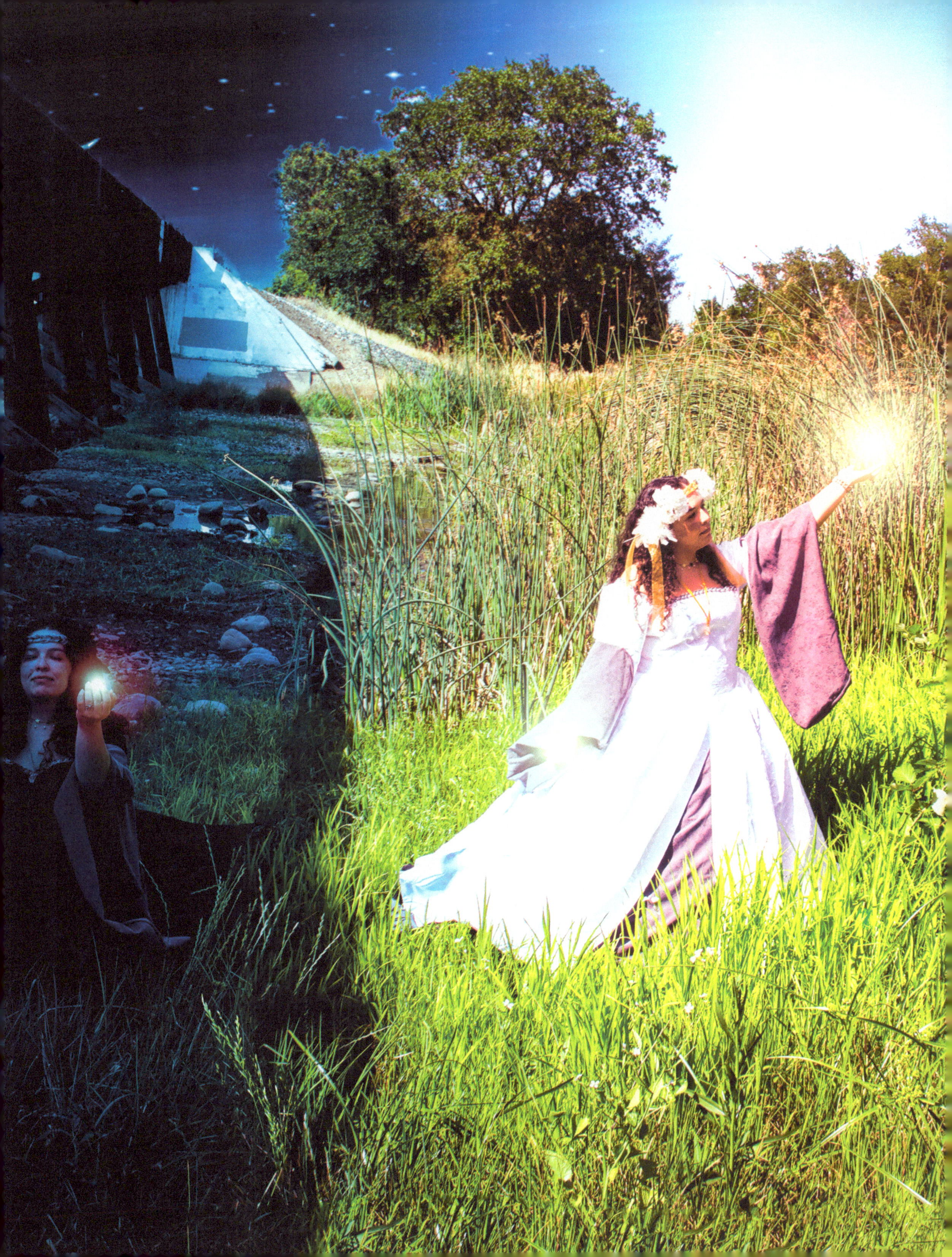

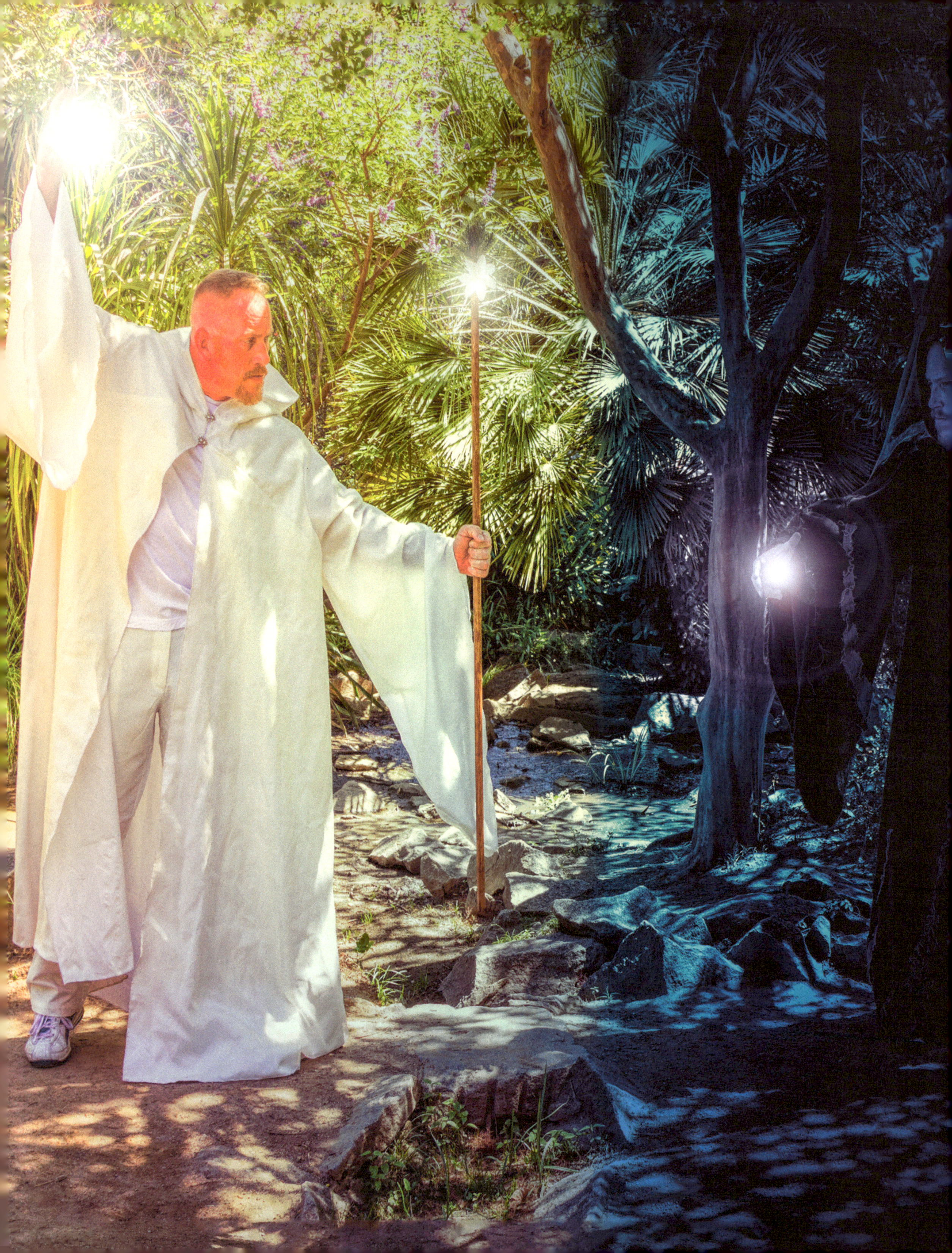

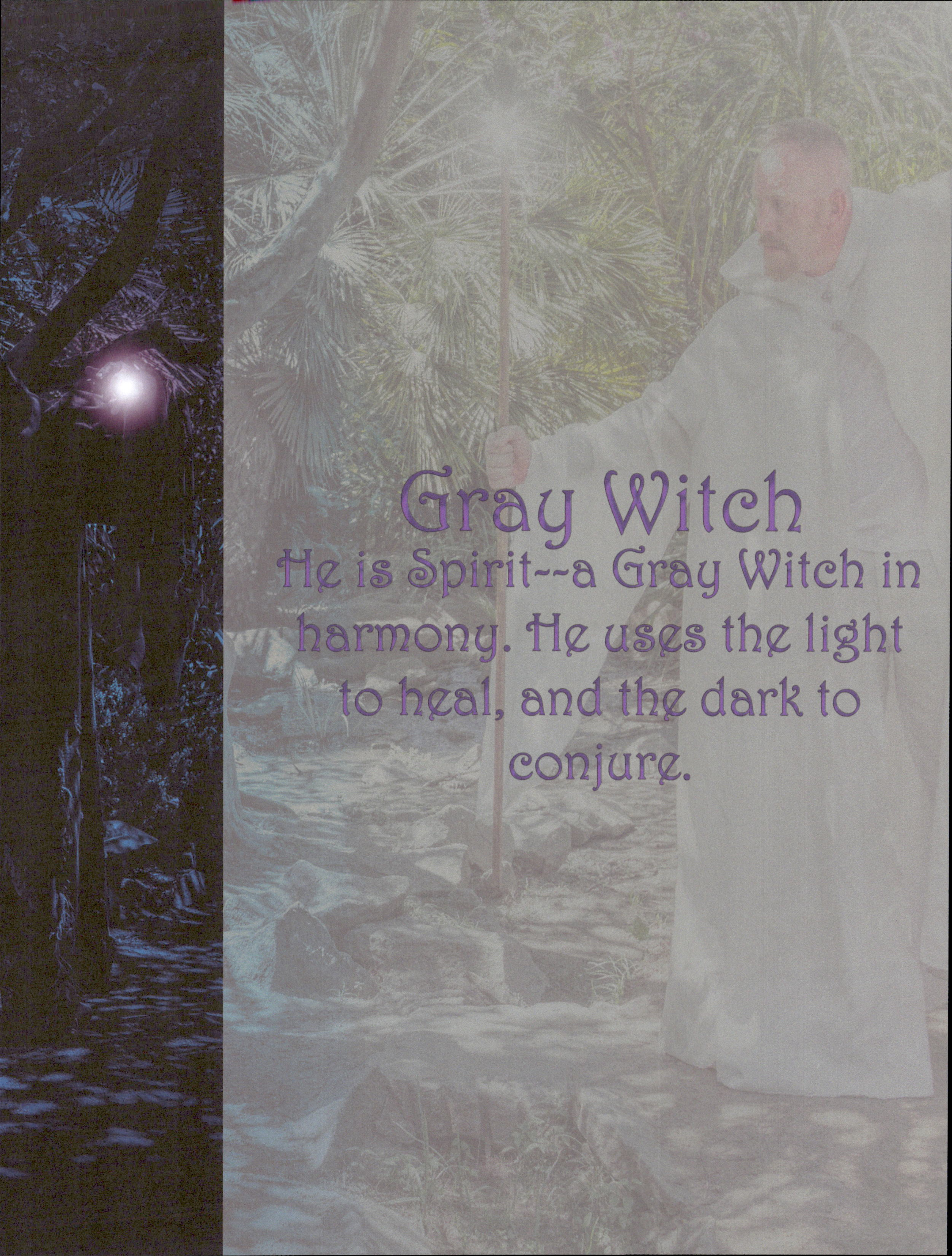

Gray Witch
He is Spirit--a Gray Witch in harmony. He uses the light to heal, and the dark to conjure.

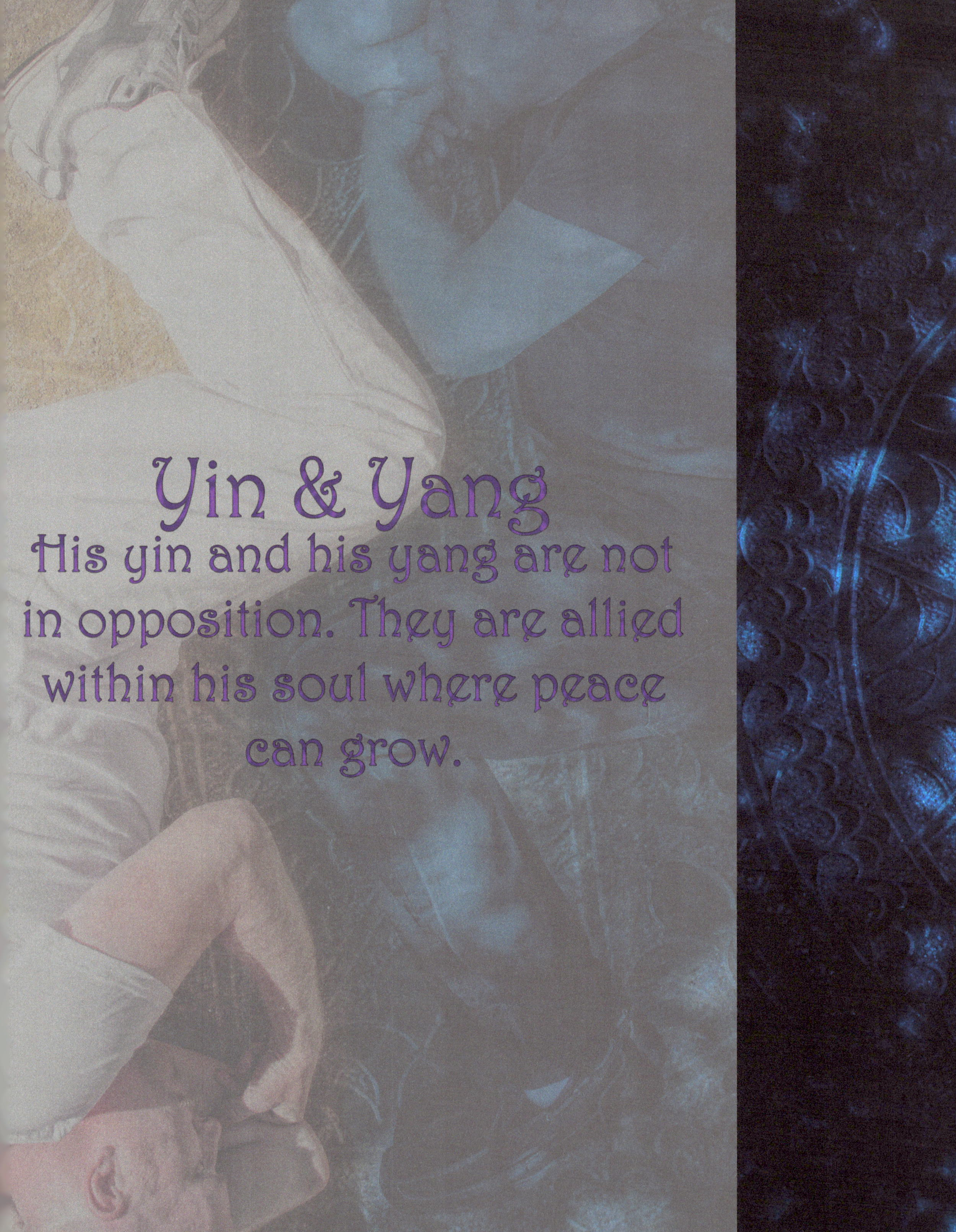

Yin & Yang
His yin and his yang are not
in opposition. They are allied
within his soul where peace
can grow.

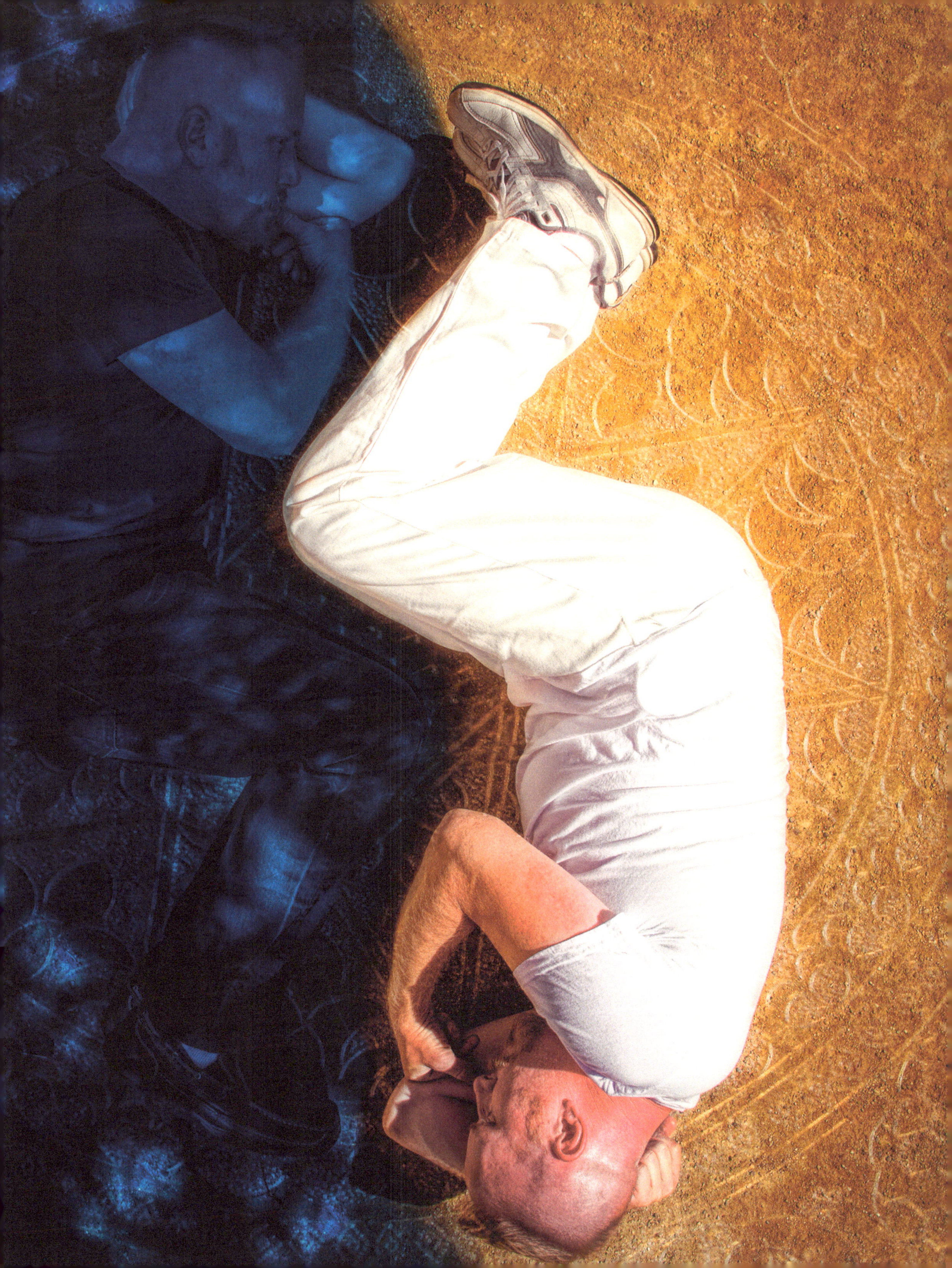

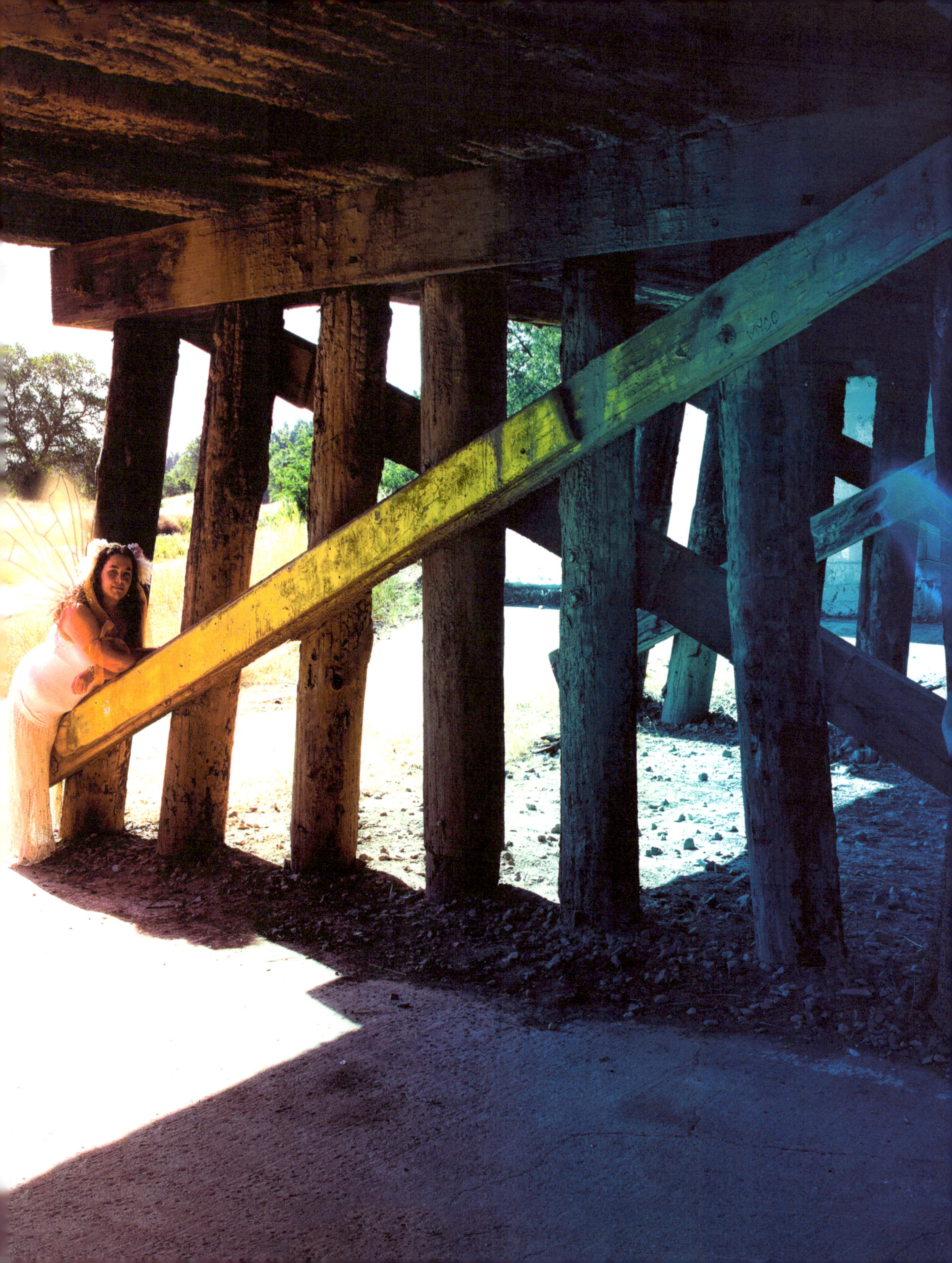

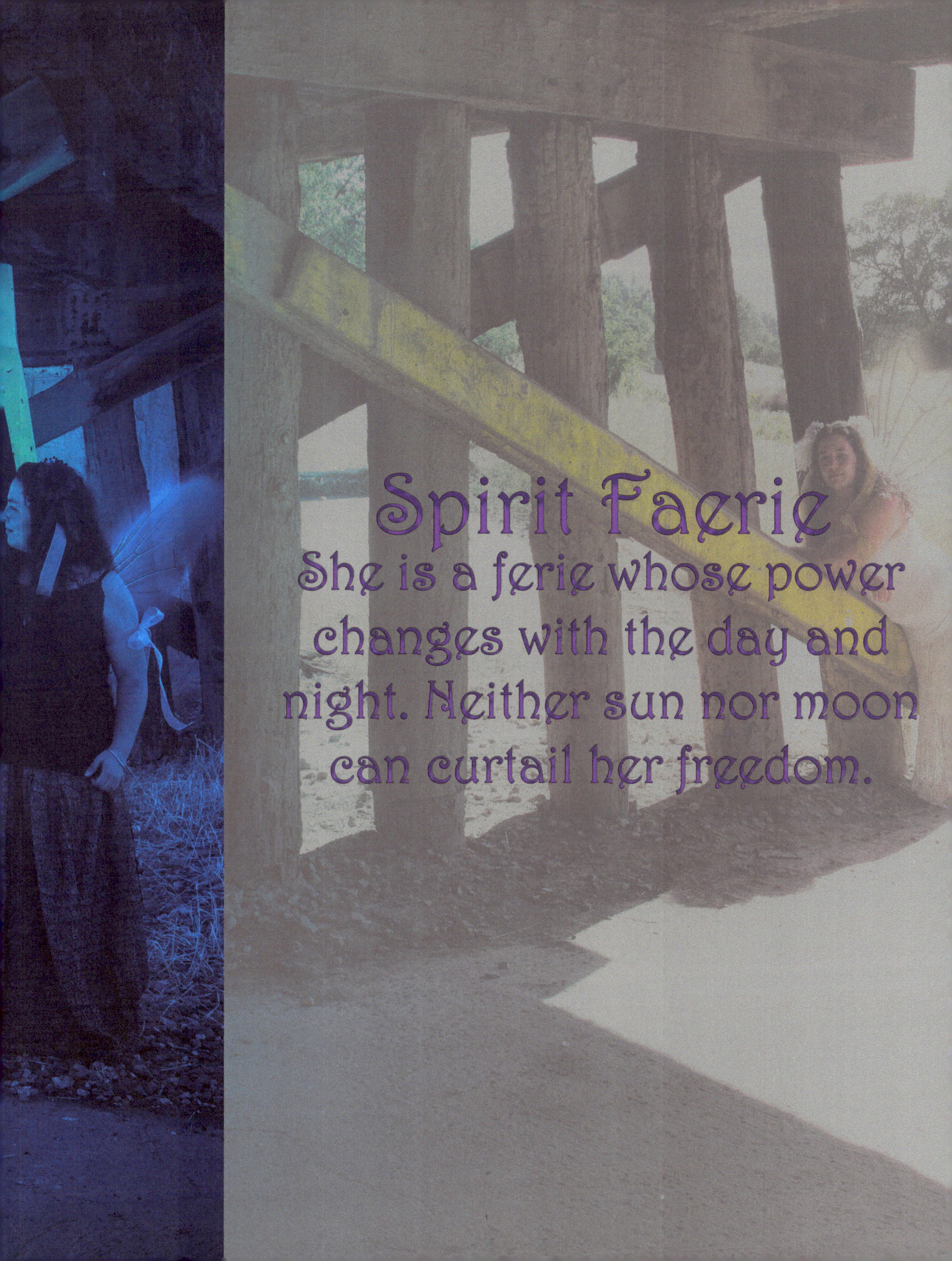
Spirit Faerie
She is a ferie whose power
changes with the day and
night. Neither sun nor moon
can curtail her freedom.

ACKNOWLEDGEMENTS

The creation of this book was truly a group effort. It was a collaborative work that could not have happened without the following people:

Theresa Vann-Stribling of Monarch Creations - Her costumes are on nearly every page. She is a sewing goddess.

Cheryl Garrett - My incredibly supportive mother who never hesitates to drive with me to strange places and puts up with the mess I make of the living room.

Sarah Lynne Klapheck - Thank you for letting me invade your yard with a rain bar and a half-naked Selkie.

All of my wonderful models - Michael, Bernadette, Lia, Sami, Laura, Kim, Megan, Rhonda, Dawn, and Clint. I hope you had as much fun making these as I did!

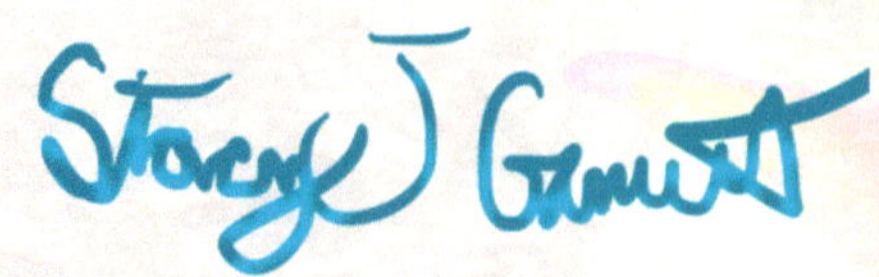

About the Photographer

Stacy J. Garrett has been a fine arts photographer since the age of twelve though she had no idea that it would be her future. A chance to take courses through the Sacramento City College's accelerated student program culminated in a position on the Honor Roll Society and an Associate of Arts Degree in Photography. She continued honing her skills by pursuing her Bachelor's Degree in Fine Arts Photography with the Academy of Art University of San Francisco and graduated in May 2016. She began the Masters of Fine Arts program in September 2016 and expects to graduate in 2019.

She considers herself extremely blessed to be surrounded by a group of amazing friends and associates who never hesitate to volunteer to do something a little strange for the sake of art, whether it is getting almost naked in a park or dressing up for a steampunk tea party.

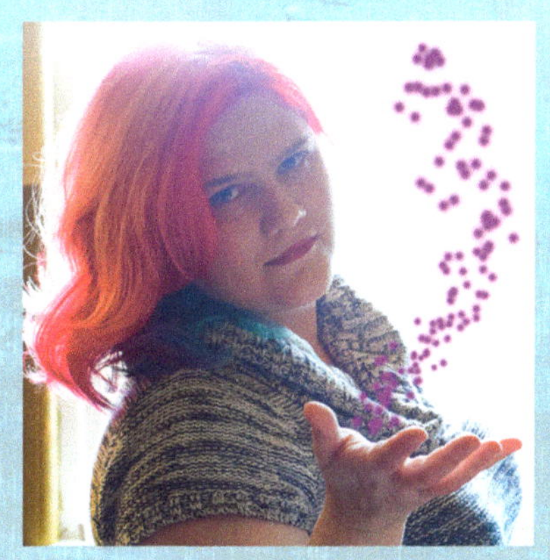